Totally Bound Publishing books by Gen Ryan

Nantucket Island
How Sweet It Is

I0607651

Nantucket Island

HOW SWEET IT IS

GEN RYAN

How Sweet It Is
ISBN # 978-1-80250-532-0
©Copyright Gen Ryan 2023
Cover Art by Kelly Martin ©Copyright April 2023
Interior text design by Claire Siemaszkiewicz
Totally Bound Publishing

HOW SWEET
IT IS

Dedication

To fond memories of summers spent on
Nantucket Island.

Chapter One

Lydia

My heels clanked against the tiled floor of City Hall, the high of the case I'd just won surging adrenaline through me. I loved my job. The hustle of a court room. The facts and research that often had to be done before a case intrigued me. Granted, having to deal with business law meant I wasn't in the court room all the time, but when I was, I won. I was two seconds away from clicking my heels together and skipping.

Landing a job at Franklin and Collins fresh out of law school was unheard of, but I had worked hard, scored an internship and proved myself early on. Early mornings. Late nights. Grunt work. I did it all. Now I wanted partner, and it was so close I could taste it. It tasted like success and victory. A small-town girl who took on the big city and succeeded. That's all I'd ever wanted since I was a little girl, and here I was, living my dream.

Smiling to myself and adjusting my briefcase, I silenced my cell phone, which hadn't stopped vibrating. I frowned when I saw who it was calling.

Home. I sighed.

Home. I hadn't been back to Nantucket since I'd left for college ten years ago. My brother Dylan and our parents still lived on the island. Dylan went into law enforcement, like my father, and worked at the local police department I laughed at the thought of all the crime he had to fight every day. Everyone knew everyone, except during the summer and tourist season, and even then, many of the same people returned to make money before college. You could drive from one end of the island to the other in less than two hours. There was one movie theater, which got movies way too late to make it even worth watching them. And they had just gotten their first Starbucks this year, which was attached to a lumber mill. My blood type was part Starbucks. I would never survive there. Not now.

The city spoke to me. The loud noises, the lights that were on at all hours. But most of all I loved that I could step foot outside of my apartment and find a little café that served coffee, tea or anything twenty-four hours a day. On Nantucket, you were lucky if the shops stayed open until five.

"Lydia!"

I spun around as Lee hustled to catch up to me.

"That was amazing. You made the defense squirm in there." He smirked, his perfect teeth almost blinding me.

"Thanks. It was a slam dunk." I tried to focus on his face, which was perfect too. With his chiseled jawline and clean-shaven smoothness. It was annoying because the way a suit looked on him always made me drool a little. I saw many men in suits in my line of work as an attorney but Lee filled his out a bit more than some with his lean muscles. We'd gone to law school together, built a solid friendship, and worked out together to let off the tension of the job. Running and lifting weights. But that was it. Our relationship was only a friendship. In my eyes, at least.

"Let's go out tonight to celebrate." Lee had asked me out many times, and while sometimes it was under the ruse of celebrating a case I'd won, or he'd won, I always said no. I didn't date. I devoted every second to my work. He knew that. It didn't stop him from trying.

"Lee, you know the answer to that." I raised my eyebrow.

"Come on. Not a date, just dinner between good friends." He reached out and squeezed my hand. My belly fluttered at the closeness of him.

And you just happen to be hot and make me want to question my no-dating rule.

My stomach growled and Lee laughed.

"See? Your stomach agrees."

I smirked at his persistent nature. I needed to eat, right?

"It'll have to be later. Like eight. I have stuff to do." I silenced my cell phone again.

"Should you get that?" he questioned.

"Just my mom again. She forgets sometimes that I'm in court most of the day." Which wasn't a lie. My mother once called me three times in a row to ask me my shirt size because she'd found the cutest sweater at a local shop that she'd known I'd just love.

Lee nodded. "Okay, so I'll pick you up at the office at eight?" He grinned. "Because I know you won't be home."

"You got it. And this isn't a date!" I called after him as he walked away.

"Right. Heaven forbid." He chuckled and waved from behind him.

Why did I say yes? I groaned and readjusted my briefcase on my shoulder. I needed food to survive. Eating was essential and something I often forgot to do until ten p.m. My stomach growled again and my phone rang. This time it was the office. I pushed aside the hunger and picked up speed to make it there quickly. This was the life I wanted. Hunger pangs, late nights and all. I wouldn't change it for the world.

* * * *

"Lydia?"

Abi, my secretary, poked her head inside my open office door. I looked up, temporarily removing my focus from the paperwork in front of me.

"I'm sorry to interrupt but your mother kept calling. Now it's your brother. I told him you're busy but he insists." She looked nervous as she fidgeted with the hem of her cardigan. Abi was my age, and while we had become close due to working together, she knew better than to interrupt me when I was busy. It was hard to get back into the zone. Especially after a conversation with my mother. It usually consisted of gossip about the town or my brother Dylan, neither of which I cared about. That was the life I'd left behind. For this.

I looked around my office, which had a killer view of downtown Boston. My mahogany desk took up much of the room and diplomas lined the wall. All of which showed that I graduated top of my class. There were no personal items in my office. That was how I liked it. I didn't like to mix business with my personal life. Many of the other attorneys had pictures of their beautiful families hanging on their walls. I didn't. It gave me a leg up. I could stay at the office as long as I needed because I didn't have recitals to go to or someone at home waiting for me.

My life was perfect and exactly how I liked it.

"You can transfer them through." I kicked off my heels, which had made my feet numb, and tucked my legs underneath myself as I continued to read case notes. I'd done many cases before, but this case had been specifically given to me by Mr. Franklin. When Franklin himself had slid this file on my desk, he'd told me he was trusting me with the reputation of his firm. I couldn't let him down.

The sound of the call coming through filled the silence of my office. I liked the silence of my office. Other than the noises that carried through sometimes from outside, I didn't listen to music because it distracted me. At only twenty-eight years old, focusing was what had gotten me this far. I wasn't the only one left at the firm right now, and everyone else was doing the same as me, trying hard to prove their worth for one of the two coveted partner spots.

"I'm going to head out. It's after five." Abi shuffled her feet. I sighed as my stomach grumbled, reminding me that I hadn't eaten since breakfast. I put down my papers and stood up. Stretching, my back made a loud cracking sound. I'd been sitting on this couch for way too long and my entire body ached.

"Go!" I waved her away "Just because I have no life doesn't mean you shouldn't," I joked. Abi laughed as she walked toward the door.

The door clicked shut and I was left alone. I padded in my bare feet to the phone and picked it up.

"Hello. This is Lydia."

"Lyd." I cringed at the nickname my brother, Dylan, had called me growing up. Well, everyone really. I had been Lyd the Kid. The youngest child born to Pearl and William Duncan. I'd been bright-eyed with light blonde hair, and I'd had a knack for arguing about everything. I'd earned my title of lawyer before I was even six years old. Everyone had known not to bother to argue with me. I'd win. Even if I was wrong.

My brother's voice sounded shaky and uneasy.

"Dylan, what's wrong?" My heart started beating rapidly.

"It's Dad. He's gone." Dylan sniffed and I clutched the side of my desk to keep myself standing upright.

"What do you mean gone? I just spoke to him last week. He was fine." There was no doubt in my mind that I was a daddy's girl. I loved that man something fierce. When I'd decided to move to Boston to pursue my education, he'd given me a wad of cash and a kiss on the forehead.

"*Live your dream, baby girl. Don't let anyone stop you.*"

And I hadn't. I'd never looked back at the small island I grew up on, or the people that I'd left behind.

"He had a heart attack this morning and was barely hanging on. Mom and I tried to get in touch with you. But…"

The guilt crept in. They had been calling me because my father was dying. The man who had never wanted anything less than for me to follow my dreams. Tears pressed against my eyes.

"I'm sorry. I didn't know. I was busy." My voice was a whisper. There was no excuse that was valid enough to miss out on my father's last breaths. Was this what regret felt like? Because I couldn't breathe. The reality that my father was gone was strangling me, and my entire mind buzzed with memories. I pulled at my dress shirt. I could have said goodbye to my father and I'd let that slip away.

I closed my eyes and forced breath into my body. My head spun and I felt like I was going to pass out. This wasn't supposed to happen this way. Both my parents were supposed to live until they were old and gray, passing peacefully in their sleep. No emergencies. Nothing sudden and catching anyone off guard. And not this young.

Boy was I naïve.

Life and Death. One wasn't promised, the other, guaranteed.

"Even Ty tried. But we know how busy you get." The mention of Ty's name made my tears fall. Ty was my brother's best friend and the man I'd thought I would marry. But when I'd left Nantucket at eighteen, Ty had decided to stay behind. He'd said he wasn't bred for the city , and that had ended our relationship. We hadn't spoken since that day. But there are just some things you don't forget about living on the island and Ty Rue was one of those things. His contagious laughter. His love of life. How he never sat still or focused. He was my antithesis. We had once been perfect for each other. But now a decade separated us, and our love was just a childhood memory. A what if. A could have been.

"Ty tried to call me?" My heart clenched. Even despite the years between us, he still tried to reach out.

Dylan sighed. "This isn't about past relationships or whatever. This is about Dad. Ty loved him too. Everyone on this island did. We need you, Lyd. Mom needs you. I need you." Dylan paused and I heard someone in the background sobbing. "God, I can't believe he's gone."

I started frantically shoving papers in my briefcase. I was knee-deep in cases and had deadlines almost every day but I wouldn't miss my father's funeral. I just hoped my job understood.

"Of course. I'll be on the late boat tonight. Will someone be able to pick me up?"

"Yeah. It'll be me or Ty. Mom's not doing too well, and I don't want to leave her alone."

My mouth went dry at the sound of his name again.

"I don't know if I can handle seeing Ty so soon."

Dylan let out a small laugh. "It's been almost ten years. Everyone's moved on. We're adults now, not teenagers falling in love with their brother's best friend."

I nodded, even though no one could see it. Of course, he'd moved on. I'd never expected Ty to stay single forever. While I didn't date, it wasn't because of Ty. It was because I was married to my job. I had everything I wanted. Yet hearing Ty's name after all these years still made me weak in the knees. He was, without a doubt, the love of my life. But sometimes you had to sacrifice one thing in order to achieve another. Ty Rune had been my sacrifice.

I may be a tough-as-nails lawyer, but I had a heart, and while I hadn't been able to get off that godforsaken island fast enough, there were times I missed the ocean breeze, my mother's home cooking, my father's laugh and Dylan's teasing. And the ice cream shop that always gave Ty, Dylan and I double scoops even when we only paid for one. And Ty. There were times I wondered what my life would be like now if we'd stayed together.

"You're right. I'll text you when I'm getting in."

Gen Ryan

"Okay. I love you, Lyd. I'm sad you're coming home under these circumstances but I'm excited to see you. It's been too long."

"I love you too. We'll get through this." The reassurance wasn't for him as much as it was for myself. I was strong, tough and could handle my emotions well. But nothing could have prepared me for the death of my father. I hadn't seen any of my family since my law school graduation years ago. My parents had come to Boston to see me walk across the stage. They'd all been so proud, holding up a huge sign with my face on it. My family had never given up on me, even though I pushed them away. I whimpered at the realization that I'd never get to tell my father how thankful I was for having him in my life.

I ended the call with Dylan and my tears took over. Falling to the ground, I sobbed for my father that I'd never get to say "I love you too" to again. For my mother, who'd lost the love of her life. And for my brother, who'd idolized that man more than anything else in the world. I didn't know how I was going to make it through this without having a full-blown breakdown. But I would be strong, like I always was, for my family. They needed me and I wouldn't let them down.

* * * *

"I'm sorry that we can't have dinner, but I appreciate you driving me all the way to the boat." Lee, my friend who wanted to be more than a friend, had offered to drive me to Cape Cod after hearing about my father's passing. It wasn't a quick drive, and I knew he had to work early in the morning.

"Don't worry about it. You're a friend and I remember how nice your family was at graduation. I'm sorry for your loss." Lee gripped my hand again for the hundredth time this trip. Every time he did I felt his expectations. He wanted more and I couldn't give it.

"Well, we made it." Lee pulled up to the dock.

"With ten minutes to spare." I looked down at Lee's hand still gripping mine. "Lee…"

"I know," he sighed. "You don't date and you want to be friends." He released my hand. "I've waited a long time for you and I won't stop now. I care about you. If you haven't noticed. So, whenever you're ready, I'll be here." Gently, he brushed a kiss to the base of my hand.

"I may never be ready," I joked as I hopped out of the car. Lee got my bag from the trunk and walked with me to the boat. While Lee was handsome and a good catch, there weren't butterflies. I may work myself into the ground but I had this fairy-tale idea of what love should feel like. Ty made me feel that.

"Guess I'll die a lonely old man." He leaned in and brushed a kiss to my cheek. "You need anything, I'm here. Don't shut everyone out, okay?"

"Hey now. That's the typical Lydia fashion. I'm better by myself."

Lee grunted.

"Whatever you say. Everyone needs someone."

Deep down I knew Lee was right. We all needed *someone*. But love and careers were often difficult, and a balancing act that I just wasn't sure I could handle. I was good at my job. That much I knew. Love? I'd known love before. I'd had the pleasure of finding someone who completed me when I was just a teenager. But that type of love? It only comes around once in a lifetime, and everything else seemed pale in comparison.

The intercom sounded, indicating final boarding for Nantucket.

"Thanks, Lee. I'll text you!" I called out as I boarded.

"I look forward to it."

I found a spot on the side of the boat so I could watch Cape Cod disappear as we taxied away. The breeze kissed my cheeks and I closed my eyes, remembering at just eighteen how I had been so excited to be leaving the island and starting my life. Now I was going home to bury my father.

Sadness enveloped me, but it was more than that. I was scared. I started shaking and wrapped my arms around myself. There was so much more that I wanted to say to everyone in my life and I never did. I just let things be because there was time. Well, time, it didn't work with us. It had its own agenda and took what it wanted whenever it pleased. Like my father. Like Ty.

What I wanted to tell Lee was that I didn't date because I had given my heart to a blue-eyed, dark-haired boy. That no one could make me feel the way he had in the short time we'd spent together. Opening my eyes, I saw that Lee still stood at the dock, his hands shoved in his pockets as he watched me drift away.

I had so many amazing people in my life that I kept at arm's length. I reminded myself that I was married to my job. That was all that there could be for me if I wanted to make partner. Sighing, I grabbed my bag and went inside. Where there was no breeze, no memories of laughter and summer kisses that made me fall in love. Just my case files and the life that I had chosen.

Chapter Two

Ty

I stirred honey into my tea and carefully balanced it on the saucer as I walked into Pearl Duncan's living room. Dylan was finishing up his phone call and I knew it was her.

Lydia.

It was hard to watch my best friend struggle to keep himself together. Losing my parents had been the worst part of my life. I had lost my mother and father a year apart about five years ago. The Duncans had been there for me. Well, all of them except Lydia. She had been off living her dream.

"Oh, honey, don't fuss over me." Pearl's eyes were red-rimmed and she clutched a tissue for dear life. Dylan flopped down on the couch next to her and it looked like he'd aged ten years in just a day.

"It's my pleasure. William was like a second father to me. Your entire family is my family." My eyes met Dylan's and he nodded, tears showing against his eyes.

Pearl started sobbing again and Dylan and I both rubbed her back.

"What am I supposed to do without the only man I've ever loved?"

I didn't know what to say to her. I wanted to tell her that she would learn to live without him. That things would get easier. But I'd experienced heartache at just twenty-one years old and never fully recovered. I'd learned to live without Lydia but there had been a part of me missing since she'd left. So I didn't say anything, because Pearl wouldn't want to hear about how she'd always miss him, no matter how much time passed.

"Is Lyd coming home?" Pearl asked as she looked expectantly at Dylan.

My heart stopped at the sound of her name. It always did. Dylan mentioned her off and on. She was his sister, after all. I'd nod and say "wow" and "amazing" when I should. But I was bitter. A man who'd let the love of his life walk away because he'd been too scared to leave the only place he knew as home — and too scared to ask her to stay.

"She is. She'll be here tonight. By the way, Ty, can you get her from the boat? She'll be in around ten." I stopped rubbing Pearl's back as all eyes were on me.

"If it's a big deal I can go. I just wanted to get things together around here. There are going to be so many people coming and going." Dylan let out a sharp breath and I could feel his anxiety rising.

"No. I'll get her. No problem." I gulped and Pearl eyeballed me. She smiled briefly before standing up and clapping her hands.

"Well, I better get cooking. Someone's got to feed all these people."

"Mom, everyone's going to bring casseroles and stuff. Isn't that what they do?" Dylan looked at me and I nodded.

"Yep. I had enough casseroles to last me a month after both Mom and Dad died."

Pearl flitted her hand like what Dylan and I were saying was nonsense. "I won't have my guests eating casseroles." She stomped out into the kitchen, soon after the sound of clanking pots and pans making its way into the living room.

"How you doing, man?" I leaned back into the couch and put my feet up on the coffee table.

"I'm okay. It's hard to believe he was just here and now he's not. I'm worried about Lyd, though. You know her. Always has to be tough and strong. Plus her job. I know she's trying to make partner."

I ground my teeth together, trying to hide my frustration. All talk about Lydia surrounded her job. It was like it was an extension of her. It seemed to be all she had become and I hated that. I knew her love for law, but she was more than that. She was a girl who'd loved the ocean, the sand between her toes. Who'd loved her family and friends and had had balance in life.

"What?" Dylan raised his eyebrow.

"Nothing," I ground out.

"Say it. I see your blood boiling over there."

"Heaven forbid she doesn't make partner," I said sarcastically.

Dylan sighed. "Don't make this hard for her. She already mentioned having a rough time and not being ready to see you."

I laughed, stood up, and started pacing the floor.

"Me? She left *me*, Dylan, remember?" I ran my fingers through my hair.

"I know, man, but she had goals and dreams that were bigger than this island. That were..." He paused and bit his lip.

"Bigger than me." I stopped pacing and looked at my best friend. The brother of the girl who stole my heart and never gave it back. Oddly, he had been okay with us dating. We'd grown up together and although we were three years older than her, I think he'd just known that we were meant to be together. Even before Lydia and I did.

"Listen, I didn't mean it like that. You're a good guy. Lydia was always bigger than this island. Everyone knew that."

"Apparently I got the memo too late. I'm going home before I have to get her from the boat."

I walked out of the Duncans' house and slammed the door. It wasn't fair to either of them. Pearl and Dylan both were grieving but the thought of seeing Lydia again, having her close to me if even temporarily, made all the memories of our childhood resurface. Who was I kidding? I played those memories through my mind often. Remembering the times when I was enough for Lydia. When our young love was sweet and pure and not yet plagued by the reality that life had brought. People moved on. Changed. Grew up. And a lot of times, they didn't grow together.

* * * *

I stood outside my truck, opting to leave the engine idling. It was cold, the chill in the brisk fall air heightened due to my proximity to the water.

People filed out of the ferry and as each hugged and kissed their loved ones, I shuffled my feet. Should I hug Lydia? Kiss her on the cheek? I was bitter, sure, but she had just lost her father. I wasn't going to let my own emotions supersede the support she needed right now.

Then I saw her, and all rational thought drifted away with the breeze. She was stunning. Refined in a way I never thought I'd see her. When I'd seen her before she'd liked worn jeans and a T-shirt, always opting for simple and comfortable. But now her pencil skirt hugged her body tightly, her heels tall and sharp as she clicked toward me. Everything faded away as I watched her blonde hair get tangled in her pink lips, then she smiled, albeit a small one, when she saw me.

"Ty." My name coming off her lips was laced with sadness that I wasn't sure was because of her losing her father or the past that we shared. I didn't care which one it was. I wanted to take away her sadness.

"Hi, Lyd. It's been a while." I opened my arms and she fell inside them, just like she used to. With a sigh, she took a deep breath.

"I'm sorry about your dad." I rubbed her back, the warmth of her body feeling like everything I'd been missing. She was comfort, friendship and love. Lydia was my everything, even after all these years.

Abruptly, she released herself from the hug, squared off her shoulders and brushed away the tears that had fallen.

"Thank you," she said, the tone of her voice turning more formal.

"Nice outfit." I grinned, taking in her spiky heels again and noticing the pearls that lined her slender neck. She was so formal and seemed so uptight. Gone was the carefree girl I had fallen in love with.

"It's what I have to wear to court, Ty. I worked today and was in court this morning." She looked me up and down.

"What happened to jeans and T-shirts?"

"I'm not that girl anymore." Lydia's eyes quickly found mine and on instinct I reached out to move the hair out of her face. She turned away and hoisted her bag into the back of my truck before I even had a chance.

"I could have gotten that." I looked at her bag.

"I can take care of myself." She slid into the front seat and I was greeted with silence as we drove away.

I turned up the music, 2000s greatest hits playing on repeat. We used to listen to this music with Dylan when we'd ride around town. I glanced out of the corner of my eye and saw the tips of her lips almost curve into a smile. Her hand tapped to the music and I grinned. The Lydia Duncan I had fallen in love with was in there still, and I'd do anything I could to bring that girl to light and to remind her of when she was my everything and that had been enough.

Chapter Three

Lydia

The last time I had been in Ty's truck we had driven to the beach for a picnic. Dylan had opted to stay behind because Ty and I had been so much in love. He'd said it got sickening sometimes watching us together. I smiled remembering Dylan making gagging sounds when Ty and I would hold hands or steal a kiss when we thought he wasn't looking.

"Are the sandwiches good?" I lay down on my stomach on the blanket we'd brought. I took off my T-shirt and showed off my new purple bikini.

"Is that new?" Ty asked.

I looked at Ty as his eyes lingered over my body.

"It is. I got it when I went to look at Boston College. God, it was so amazing, Ty." I sat up and tucked my legs underneath me. "I wish you could see it. The big campus. All the shopping and stores. And they have a Starbucks! It's the best coffee I ever tasted." I was talking so fast Ty laughed.

"Sounds like it's everything you dreamed." He tucked a piece of hair behind my ear and smiled at me.

"It is with you by my side. Did you apply to college around there yet? It doesn't matter which one, I can commute or you can. We can get an apartment. There are so many and public transportation, it's so convenient." I took a bite of my sandwich.

Ty sighed and looked down at the blanket.

"What?" I put my sandwich on the plate.

"I'm not sure I want to go to college."

"You want to just work? That's fine. Boston has lots of jobs." I shrugged.

"I'm not sure I want to go to Boston. I want to stay here." He looked out at the ocean. The sound of the waves crashing against the rocks, a familiar sound that usually soothed me, now made me uneasy. My heart dipped. He didn't want to come with me?

"But why?"

"Why not?" He pointed to the water. *"I love it here. The beach is only a short drive or walk away. Everyone knows everyone. We talked about opening a candy shop, remember? Maybe I'll do that."*

I scoffed. Candy shop?

"We aren't going to be children forever, Ty. Those were dreams we talked about when there was nothing better."

"So what? I don't want to become a big-shot lawyer so I'm not good enough anymore?"

"It's not that. You know I don't care what you do. But staying here? What does Nantucket have to offer that Boston doesn't?" I crossed my arms across my chest.

Ty reached out and took my hand in his. *"It always had you. Dylan. My family and friends. It's peace and tranquility. It's my home."*

"Well it won't have me anymore. I've been accepted to Boston College and I'm going." I stood up and gathered my T-shirt and shoes.

"That's it then?" Ty stayed seated and picked at his sandwich.

"Guess so." Tears fell down my cheeks as I walked away. I kept looking back, hoping that Ty would be close behind me, but he never came. He let me go and I left and never looked back.

I had left for college without saying goodbye to Ty. Dylan had said he was upset and I had been too stubborn to go to him. We both were to blame for how things ended. Two stubborn kids in love and not knowing what to do.

"Home sweet home," Ty said as he pulled up the driveway of my childhood home. All houses on Nantucket looked the same on the outside with their gray shingles. The makeup of the wood protected them from the salty sea air. But my house always took my breath away. It wasn't big and overbearing like some of the other homes on the island. We weren't a rich family by any means. It was a modest cottage home with three bedrooms and one bathroom. It was what was inside that always made me feel so warm and rich. Richer than any of the celebrities that came here to vacation. I had a family that loved me. And I loved them.

"Thanks for getting me. I'm sure that there were other things you could have been doing." Okay, I sounded like I was fishing for information, and sue me, but I was. I wanted to know all that I had missed out on in the past ten years. Who was Ty? What did he do? Had he fallen in love with someone and forgotten all about me? About us?

He let out a staggered breath and pinned his eyes on me.

"What do you want to know, Lyd? I see it in your eyes." He laughed. "You always had such expressive eyes."

"I realized we haven't seen each other in ten years." I fiddled with my skirt.

"Yeah, it's been a while." Ty turned down the music.

"So, I just didn't know what you do now. How you are. That's all." I grabbed my purse so I could make a quick getaway. The air in the truck was stifling. I couldn't be here with him. It made me feel what it had been like when we were so in love. I hadn't felt that way in a long time.

"I'm the same guy I was ten years ago. Just a few gray hairs." He ruffled his hair, which didn't look like it had a single gray in it. He was different. What he didn't know was his eyes had always captivated me. Drawn me in. Just like the ocean, threatening to swallow you whole at any moment. In his eyes was sadness and loss, each time he looked at me, and it killed me. I'd done that to him. I'd broken Ty's heart.

"I'll see you tomorrow?" I opened the door and held it open. I wasn't sure what I was waiting for. For him to hold me back? To tell me that he'd never stopped thinking about me? My mind felt like mush and I hated it. I wanted the structure of contracts and business law. I could count on that. Love? Emotions? Those pesky buggers made no sense at all. Why after ten years did Ty still bring me to my knees?

"Yeah. I have a few things to take care of in the morning but I'll be around for Dylan."

"Right." *For Dylan.* I wasn't included with them anymore because I'd left. They'd only had each other all these years. Where it used to be Dylan, Ty and Lyd, It was just Dylan and Ty now.

Ty hopped out of the truck and grabbed my bag for me, bringing it up to the front of the house and dropping it on the doorstep.

"Goodnight." He turned on his heels and walked away, leaving me with a heart and mind that were so confused.

The front door opened and there stood my brother. "Lyd?" One look at him was all it took for me to lose it. He brought me against his chest and I grabbed at his shirt and sobbed.

"I didn't even get to say goodbye. Or tell him how much I loved him."

"*Shh*. He knew," Dylan soothed. "He knew how much you loved him."

His words might have been true but the guilt still threatened to strangle me. I'd never forgive myself for ignoring those calls today. I'd missed the chance to say goodbye to my father because I'd been too wrapped up in my life to care about anyone else.

* * * *

"Do you always work at two a.m.?" My mother pulled her robe tighter around her body and frowned at the open window.

"Leave it open, please. I missed the ocean breeze." I didn't even look up from my laptop.

"Did you just say you missed something about the island you couldn't get far enough away from?" She chuckled as she sat down next to me.

"Ha ha. I didn't run. I went to college. Big difference."

"Fair enough." She looked down at the table, her red-rimmed eyes looking worse than earlier.

"Hard time sleeping?" I asked, temporarily leaving my work.

"Yeah. It's hard without your father next to me. I got so used to it, you know?"

"I can only imagine, Mom." I reached out and took her hand in mine.

"I have tons of life insurance paperwork and other stuff that I have to go through. I know you're busy but I figured you'd know how to decipher most of it better than I can." She sniffed.

"Of course, Mom. You don't even have to ask. I'm here for you."

Her eyes averted to my laptop.

"Seems like you brought a lot of work with you." She patted the stack of papers.

"This is nothing compared to what some weeks look like. My boss approved two weeks away from the office but I have to work while I'm here. It's my job. My life." I shrugged.

My mother looked at me sadly and stood up.

"As long as you're happy. I'm going to try to get a few more hours of sleep before people start filing in offering condolences."

"And casseroles," I said with a giggle.

She cringed. "Hate casseroles." Leaning in, she placed a kiss to my forehead. "I'm glad you're home, sweetie."

"Me too." I watched as she headed to her bedroom, her words replaying in my mind.

"As long as you're happy."

I stared at the stack of papers and rubbed my eyes. I *was* happy. This was all I'd ever dreamed of. I'd given up everything to become a lawyer. It had to be enough.

Refocusing, I continued typing out the fifth contract.

* * * *

Closing my laptop at five a.m., I changed into my running outfit and laced up my sneakers. I needed to clear my mind. As soon as my feet hit the pavement, it was as if everything fell into place. The salt air greeted me and my feet knew the route they normally took.

I was home.

I ran the familiar route to downtown, the town still sleeping as I ran past all the stores that I'd once frequented. I started walking, smiling as I saw that not much had changed.

Stopping in front of a colorful store, I looked up and gasped.

How Sweet It Is — Candy Store

Ty and I had danced to *How Sweet It Is*, swaying side to side, at prom. My big poufy dress had had its own area code but I hadn't cared. I'd felt like a princess, and I'd had the tiara to match.

"I'm going to open a candy store one day and name it How Sweet It Is."

I giggled. "Why?"

"Because it's sweet being loved by you, Lyd." He spun me around and I laughed as he brought me close against him.

"Careful, I might give you a cavity."

He groaned. "You've been listening to Dylan's corny jokes too long."

I tilted my head back and laughed.

Dylan winked at us as he slow danced with his date. Resting my head against Ty's chest, I smiled and knew that nothing could tear us apart. Ty was it for me and always would be.

I stared at the candy store and knew that it was Ty's. He was living his dream, just like I was living mine. While that should have brought me comfort, it didn't. Because I remembered what it was like being loved by him, and it was the greatest feeling in the world. I wondered if he remembered what being loved felt like. Looking at the candy shop, the bright colors and deliciousness gleaming in the storefront window, I knew he did too.

Tightening my shoelace, I did what I did best—I ran.

Chapter Four

Ty

"Hey, Ty. Didn't expect you this early." Kara, the barista at Starbucks, smiled widely. I was pretty sure she'd been flirting with me for the past month but I was about as oblivious to flirting as they came. I often mistook a wink for an eye infection.

"Just here to get a few things for the Duncans before I head over."

Her face softened as she reached out and patted my hand.

"I didn't know William well but he was always such a nice guy when he came in here. Even if he was ranting about chain stores coming to his island." Kara had only been in town for a few months. She'd helped open the Starbucks and was here most days.

I laughed. "That's William. He's a great guy." I cleared my throat and corrected myself. "*Was* a great guy." The thought of William not coming in every Friday for his bag of candy tugged at my heart. There were a lot of things I loved about living on Nantucket, but that was one of my favorites—the people who touched your life and were a part of it every day. A constant. Unwavering. There whenever you needed them.

"If you need anything I'm here for you." She smiled.

A clearing of the throat interrupted us and Kara glanced around me.

"I'm sorry, miss, can I help you?"

I looked back and ripped my hand from Kara's when I saw Lydia standing there, her arms crossed across her chest as she stared daggers at Kara.

"Am I interrupting?" Lydia asked.

Kara blushed and I stepped aside so Lydia could order.

"Not all. I was here to get a few things to bring to your house. What's your poison? Tell Kara here. She makes a mean cup of coffee!" I tried to lighten the mood. Lydia looked like she was about to jump across the counter.

"Oh stop!" Kara giggled.

Lydia rolled her eyes before placing her order.

"I'll take nonfat caramel macchiato. Skim milk, please." She motioned for me to order.

"Black coffee. And I'll take a few assorted pastries, please."

Kara scurried away, but not before taking one last glance at me. She winked. Eye infection or flirting? *Yeah, she was flirting.*

"No wonder she makes a mean cup of coffee, if you drink it black." Lydia smirked.

"You're sounding a little jealous." I leaned against the counter and grinned at her. I caught her glancing down at my arms, which pressed against my sweater.

Was Lydia Duncan checking me out? Now this I could easily misjudge. I wanted her to look at me. To remember what it had been like when we were together, because we had been so great.

"Jealous of her?" Lydia laughed. "You must be mistaken."

"I remember you were always jealous. Any girl who showed me attention you'd fight off with a stick."

"I think you're making that up." Lydia stuffed some napkins in her purse.

"Marie. Prom. When she asked me for a dance you practically bit her hand off."

Lydia smiled and shook her head.

"The girls at the beach who would look at my muscular bod as I put on sunscreen. You'd kiss me senseless to stake your claim."

Heat rushed to Lydia's cheeks. She remembered how it felt to kiss me. I knew she did. Truth was, I'd never forgotten how it felt to kiss her.

"Point proven, but I've grown up since then."

I glanced over her body, noticing the lovely yoga pants that hugged her just right. Her once youthful body had been replaced with one that could only be described as full woman and glorious.

"I noticed."

"Ahem." Kara stood in front of us with a package of pastries and two drinks. "Here you go. That'll be thirty-two fifty."

Lydia went to pull out her card but I beat her to it.

"Oh, come on, Ty, I can pay for my family's food."

"They're my family too," I said as Kara handed me some change.

Taking her coffee, Lydia looked at me and nodded. We walked out in silence to the parking lot.

"Did you walk here?" I noticed only my truck and Kara's small car in the parking lot.

"Yeah. I ran downtown this morning and ended up here." She held the coffee in her hands and breathed it in.

"Let me drive you home." I held the passenger-side door open and she looked between the door and me a few times.

"Fine." She sighed before getting in.

"You act like I bite," I joked as I placed the food in the back seat before sliding into the front.

"You've only ever treated me with kindness. It's not that."

"Then what is it?" I turned down the music that I always blared through town. People knew I was coming from a mile away.

"Nothing. Let's go. I'm sure my mom is wondering where I am. And work. I need to call in before my boss freaks out."

I wanted to peel back the layers of Lydia that had grown over the years. Before she'd left we had been able to talk effortlessly. Now everything seemed forced and she seemed so distant. I guess that was to be expected with ten years between us.

"Okay. I'll take you home." And that's exactly what I did. In silence.

* * * *

We pulled up to her house and she groaned at the cars that lined the driveway.

"It's not even nine a.m. yet," she complained.

"Small town." I shrugged as I got the pastries out of the back seat.

"I forgot what it was like."

"What?" I quirked my eyebrow as we walked to the front door.

"Being from a small town. Boston is different." She took a sip of her coffee.

"What's it like?"

"Loud. People everywhere. Cars honking. But there's a Starbucks on every corner and things are open twenty-four-seven. It's different here."

"Better than here?" I balanced the food on my hip and opened the door with my free hand. Lydia held the coffees and looked at me, offering a sad smile.

"Different. Not better or worse. You should come visit sometime. I'd love to show you around."

I looked up before I could respond and Dylan stood in front of us, his eyebrows furrowed.

"Your phone has been ringing nonstop. I answered and about took the head off some girl named Abi. Our father died and they can't even give you some space?"

Lydia looked frantic as she rushed to the kitchen, Dylan and me trailing behind her. Placing down the coffees, she gave Dylan a hug.

"They only know deadlines and contracts. I'd better give them a call." She slipped out of Dylan's arms and he shook his head as she snatched her phone off the table and scurried away.

People milled around. Women sipping tea at the table looked at me and smiled.

"What was that about?" Dylan opened the Starbucks package and took a huge bite of a chocolate donut.

"What?" I asked.

"You and Lyd showing up here together?"

"She ran this morning and we happened upon each other at Starbucks. I gave her a ride home. That's it." I held up my hands in defense.

"You still love her." Dylan said it as a fact, not a question. The chatter at the table was a whisper as the women tried to listen.

"I never stopped." I swear I heard a few of them say 'aww'. I glared at them and they pretended they were talking. This would be on the five o'clock news.

Headline—Ty Rue still loves Lydia Duncan.

"Bring her home, Ty." Dylan slapped my shoulders.

"She left me before. What makes you think she'll stay this time? She has an entire life in Boston."

Dylan shook his head and finished off the donut. "Something seems different. She says she's happy but I know my sister. She still loves you too."

I let out an exaggerated breath as Lydia bounced by and swiped a glazed donut, her cell phone clutched to her ear. Some things never changed and obviously her love of sweets hadn't.

"Donut? Yet you ordered a nonfat skim milk coffee thing?" I laughed.

Lydia stopped and stuck out her tongue at me. Laughing, she walked away.

Glancing at the clock, I realized I had to open the store in a few minutes.

"I've got to go open the store. I'll be back over tonight."

"Dinner's at six. I'm not sure what's going on, but that's what I've been told."

I laughed and gave Dylan a quick hug. "You need anything you call me, got it?"

"Yeah. Go sell candy to little kids." He waved me away.

I grinned. "You got it!"

I made it to How Sweet It Is in just minutes. As soon as I unlocked the front door, the smell of chocolate and peppermint welcomed me. I switched the sign from closed to open and settled in behind the desk.

The door jingled open and in walked Mrs. Abbott, one of the oldest residents of the island.

"Morning, dear."

"Morning, Mrs. Abbott."

She slowly walked through the aisles like she did every morning, picking up various pieces of candy and taffy, even though she would get the same thing every day, peppermint patties.

As I rang her out I noticed she was staring at me more than usual.

"I heard Lydia is back." She glanced at me as she shuffled through her bag, which was big enough to hold a body in.

"She is."

"Heard you two were seen driving around this morning." Mrs. Abbott didn't bother looking at me.

I sighed. News traveled fast.

"We were. We had coffee and I brought her home before opening this morning."

"Excellent. I always knew you two would end up together."

She slapped a twenty-dollar bill on the counter and scurried off before I could defend myself.

"Keep the change!" she yelled as the door slammed shut.

That woman may be pushing eighty, but when she wanted to move she sure could. I knew I probably should give Lydia a heads-up about the gossip that was already going around. She hadn't even been here twenty-four hours. The door jiggled opened again and a few out-of-towners came in, oohing and awing at the nostalgic old candy that made up the majority of the store.

There was nothing like old candy to bring back memories of people's childhoods. When times were simpler and love was as easy as giving the girl you liked a Ring Pop and getting married in the backyard. I smiled, remembering Dylan standing as my best man when I was just eight years old and his sister was five. We'd had a pretend wedding and I'd placed a Ring Pop on Lydia's little finger. She'd squealed because it was green, her favorite. Then she'd placed a red one on my finger, and I knew then that one day I'd marry her. Because red was my favorite.

Guess life had other plans.

Laughing, I helped the family navigate through the store and pick out candy and make new memories that they would cherish forever. The kids filled their baskets high as the parents held hands and spoke softly and lovingly to each other.

Memories were all I had now. Of times when me, Lydia and Dylan had been friends taking over the world. Now it was just Dylan and me. Living out our dreams on an island that had never been enough for Lydia. But those memories, I'd cherish them forever. Just like I would her. The girl that stole my heart with a Ring Pop.

Chapter Five

Lydia

Shoving the stack of papers that my mother had handed me under my arm, I snuck away to my bedroom. I loved that my parents hadn't changed my room since I'd left. Dylan still lived at home, so his room was slightly more mature, but mine still had boy band posters on the walls and the shelves were lined with the law books that I had collected in my teenage years. Running my fingers over the books, I blew on the books, dust flying into the air. It'd been a long time since I'd been home.

Laying on my full-size bed, I began to scour through the documents my mother was too overwhelmed to look over. My father's entire life was in this pile, many of the documents going back to before Dylan and I were even born. Their marriage license, our birth certificates, locks of our hair. A few scattered pictures flitted out. I laughed at Dylan and I, who were cheesing as we hugged each other.

I stopped in the middle of the stack, a lot of the stuff up until now being mostly memories held in a box. But this document, it was my father's wishes. He wanted to be cremated. My mind whirled with thoughts and emotions that I hadn't even known would surface. I'd never thought that he would want anything other than a normal funeral. There'd be a wake and a pastor who would say what a good man he was as they lowered his body into the ground. People would cry and place roses on his coffin.

There would be none of that.

I ran out into the kitchen, ignoring the few stragglers who were still hovering over my mother.

"Did you know that Dad wanted to be cremated?" I clutched the paper tighter in my hand.

My mother nodded.

"Dylan, did you?" I turned around to see my brother heating up dinner — pasta and homemade sauce someone had brought over.

"Everyone did, Lyd."

I sucked in a sharp breath.

"Everyone but me," I said out loud. The ladies who were sitting at the table shuffled awkwardly in their seats, their chairs scraping the floor.

"You're never home. We didn't want to bother you with that kind of stuff. Your father didn't want people fussing over him. He wanted to be cremated and his ashes spread on the beach, the place he loved the most," my mom said as she looked up at me.

My palms got sweaty and my mind couldn't quite process everything she was saying. I understood that these were his wishes but I was heartbroken. Where would I go to visit my father? There'd be no gravestone or place for me to mourn. My father would just be gone. And I had no say in anything.

I slammed the paper down on the kitchen table and my mother jumped, her sobs ringing loud and clear in my ears. Dylan placed his hand on my shoulder and I brushed him off.

"Stop." I backed away as everyone stared at me. I was coming unhinged. No one needed to see this. Heck, I didn't even want to see it. "I just need some time alone right now." Ripping my sweater off the coat rack, I quickly left and walked to the place that brought me peace, the beach.

The air was chilly. Way too chilly for just the thin sweater I'd grabbed before I'd stormed out of the house. I was ashamed of how I'd acted. My mother and brother didn't deserve my anger. I spoke out loud, hoping that wherever my father was he could hear me.

"Dad, I understand why you did it. You loved the water. I remember when you took us to this very beach as kids." I let the sand seep through my fingers. It was cold, like the breeze, and I swear I heard my father's laughter. "God, I miss you so much. I'm sorry I wasn't here. I'm so sorry." The breeze brushed away my tears and I fought with my emotions. I hated feeling so weak and out of control. I never would have thought that I would have been able to storm out like I had.

Out of the corner of my eye, I saw Ty slink down next to me. We sat in silence for a while, just watching the waves and listening to the sea gulls as they flew overhead. A few of them dipped into the water, scooping up their dinner.

"How'd you know I was here?" I ran my fingers through the sand again.

"It's where you used to always come when we were younger and you were upset." Ty said it like it was a fact. And it was. This was the spot I'd go to when Dylan or my parents made me mad. This was where I'd gone when Ty hadn't followed me after our picnic. He'd never come to see me. He'd let me go.

"Are Dylan and Mom totally pissed at me?" I glanced over at him and he shrugged.

"No. Everyone's just worried about you."

"Worried why?" I scrunched up my nose.

"Really, Lyd? You always try to be strong. You put on this brave face like you can tackle the world. I know you. Inside of you is an emotional girl who thinks way too much and analyzes everything. It's okay to feel."

I let out a small laugh. "The last time I felt anything I got my heart broken. Now look at me. I'm a mess. A twenty-eight-year-old woman who can't even come to terms with her father's death."

Ty played with the sand as he dissected my words.

"Did I miss dinner?"

Ty nodded. "But Dylan left us both plates. He had to go into work for a bit. Your mom went to bed."

"It's only seven," I said as I glanced at my cell phone.

"I know. She had a rough day."

"I had a rough day too." I looked over at Ty and his eyes softened.

"I know. Do you want to talk about it?" he asked as he tried to brush back my hair, which was getting tangled in the ocean breeze.

"Not yet. I just wish I couldn't feel any of it. It hurts so bad."

Ty brought his arms around me and my head fell onto his shoulder.

"When will it get better?" I looked up at him expectantly. I wanted him to tell me that it would all get better. That the constant ache in my chest of missing my father would go away.

"When I lost my parents it was the hardest years of my life. It gets easier, I guess. Not better. You don't stop missing them, but the pain isn't so poignant."

I couldn't find anything to say to him. I hadn't come home when Ty's mother had passed. Or when his father had passed a year later. I'd sent my once best friend a bouquet of white roses and a card that said, "my greatest sympathy in your time of mourning". So impersonal. I hadn't been there for him when he'd needed me.

Yet he was here with me and my family. Holding me like I had never left him all those years ago. Guilt overcame me again. This time it wasn't for not getting to say goodbye to my father, but for letting Ty go through the loss of not one but both of his parents alone.

"I'm so sorry, Ty."

"For what?" Ty looked down at me.

"I didn't come home when your parents passed. I can only imagine. I have Dylan but you had —"

"No one?" Ty let out a small laugh and stood up, brushing sand off his clothes. "Dylan and your parents were there for me. This town was there for me. That's one of the many reasons I stayed here. Because this island would never turn their backs on me when I needed them the most." His chest heaved with his words, which I knew were targeted at me. The anger that burned in his eyes further ignited the emotions that were threatening to take over.

"I'm going home. I'll text Dylan that I'm sorry for missing dinner." Ty stormed away, leaving me in the one place where I could go to compose my thoughts and get grounded. Suddenly the regret of everything I'd done to lead me to this very moment threatened to drown me. My guilt and regret dragging me down to the ocean floor.

If only it was that easy. Instead, I'd have to learn to deal with this pain and loss, and the broken heart that had never healed all these years. I'd have to learn to let go.

Chapter Six

Ty

I sat alone at the bar just like, according to Lydia, I was in my actual life. I had forgotten how infuriating she could be. But that was one of the many things I loved about her — the way she could argue any point. Even if she was wrong, you'd lose because she was that good. I hadn't been surprised when she'd started getting interested in becoming a lawyer. She was made for that kind of work, just like I was made to open a candy store and stay on this island.

Where had that gotten us when we'd fallen in love? Heartbroken. Two people from the same world, growing in opposite directions. It put distance and time between us when we'd needed to hold on to the little things that had made us fall in love in the first place. Like this island. With its cobblestones that made it hard to drink coffee and drive. The stores that closed at five p.m. because it was important that everyone made it home in time for dinner with their families. And the people, that while they often were nosey and knew your business before you even did, they were also close and fiercely protective of everyone who lived here.

"Do you want another?" Justin, the bartender, asked. His family owned the bar and he took care of most of the day-to-day operations. His parents were older and what we called snowbirds. They lived on the island during the summer and headed to Florida during the winter. Justin took care of things while they were gone. I was glad he'd decided to move here because he was a good guy. Dylan and I hung out with him sometimes, and it was nice to just sit back and chat with the boys.

"You know one's my limit." I took a long swig of my beer and wiped my mouth on the back of my hand.

"All right, what's going on? You're always in here for your one beer, but that look on your face... It's a look only a woman could put there." Justin chuckled.

"Sounds like you're speaking from experience." I frowned. Justin had moved here permanently a few years back after a bad breakup. He never talked much about it, but the way he avoided the topic it was clear it had messed him up big time.

"Yeah. I didn't move from Texas to Nantucket on a whim." Justin's voice got lower, making the sadness of the breakup seemingly fresh.

"It's Lydia."

"That's Dylan's sister, right? I never met her. I wasn't one of the cool kids who were raised on the island." He chuckled as he continued to dry glasses and put them away.

"Yeah, Dylan's sister. The love of my life who broke my heart and left me behind." I took in a sharp breath.

"Sucks but there it is. Now she's back and she's different. Boston changed her. Being a lawyer changed her."

Justin put the glass down and leaned on the bar.

"You know what I learned? That people change. It sucks but it's a part of life. I'm sure you changed too. Can't expect either of you to be the same people you were when you were younger." He pushed back, off the bar. Grabbing two beers, he popped off the caps and slid one in front of me and took a sip out of the other.

"You're drinking with me? That's a first."

"All this love stuff gives me hives. Makes me remember the reason I came here in the first place." He took a long pull of his beer.

"Women." Justin and I clicked bottles even though I had no intention of drinking a second. Justin polished his off quickly, letting out a small burp.

"I love her, though. I can't stop thinking about her since I picked her up off that boat. Who am I kidding? I haven't stopped thinking about her in ten years."

Justin nodded, took my beer out of my hand and took a drink, the weight of our conversation seemingly impacting him.

"Tell her. Don't be like me and give it all up because things got hard. You guys grew up together. Deep down there's a familiarity there that never goes away."

I took in Justin's words, and I knew he was right. The thing with Lydia and me was that we never had trouble expressing ourselves. Sometimes we were *too* expressive. But what I could do was remind her of all that Nantucket once meant to her. All that *I* once meant to her.

"Do you miss her? The girl you left behind?" I asked.

Justin looked at me, tossing the beer bottles in the recycling. "Every day, man. Every day."

I threw some money on the bar and said my goodbyes. Tired didn't begin to explain how I felt. It was only a little after nine, but tomorrow would be an early morning, as some items I'd ordered were coming in on the early boat. Which meant I had to drag all the product to the store, unpack it and inventory it. That was my least favorite part of the job. But seeing people's faces when they walked into the store and saw the various types of old candy mixed in with the new made it all worth it.

* * * *

My doorbell rang and I shot off the couch, tripping over my shoes and nearly breaking my neck. I swung the door open as I tried to get my T-shirt on.

"Were you sleeping? I'm so sorry." Lydia ducked her head as I finished putting on my shirt. She shoved a Tupperware container at me as she kept her gaze averted.

"No. I was just dozing on the couch. What's this?" I held the container away from me to try to get a peek at what was inside.

"The pasta from tonight. I felt bad how we ended things on the beach and worried whether you had eaten." She bit her bottom lip.

"It's way past dinner." I chuckled. "But thank you for thinking of me."

Lydia's eyes twinkled and I finally got a chance to look at what she was wearing. Just jeans and a hoodie. Like old times.

"You look nice." I held the door open wider, making a gesture for her to come in.

"This?" She laughed as she tugged on her hoodie that said "How Sweet It Is" on it. "My mom gave it to me since I packed mostly work clothes. Congratulations by the way, on opening your store." She stepped inside my house and suddenly everything shifted. The air stilled and the scent of her sweet perfume enveloped me. She smelled even better than peppermint and chocolate. It was delicate and subtle, like honey and lemons mixed together.

"Thanks. Seems like we both followed our dreams, huh?" There was so much more that I wanted to say. That after she'd left for Boston I had barely been able to get out of bed, let alone think of opening the store. But after my parents had died, and with the life insurance money they'd left me, I'd made my dream a reality. Someday, I'd hoped, she'd come back and see the store and remember that night at prom. Because it was sweet to be loved by Lydia. Almost as sweet as it was to love her. Even though she hadn't been here for me physically when my parents died, it was that night at prom, really, all the nights we'd shared together, that had brought me out of my depression at losing my parents.

Lydia moved around the living room, stopping at all the pictures that lined the walls. I had moved into my parents' house when they'd passed and hadn't really changed much.

"Oh, my goodness. Look at us!" Lydia laughed as I walked over to see which picture she was talking about. Dylan, Lydia and I were on the beach, probably no one older than fifteen. My eyes were pinned on Lydia, who was grinning from ear to ear as she held a huge crab in her hand. *Even then I couldn't keep my eyes off her.*

"We were so young." Lydia stared at the photo. She looked the same as in the photo, her smile wide as she remembered when we were all together. When things were simpler, when our dreams were distant and not yet a reality and nothing could tear us apart.

Our eyes met and for the first time since that day on the beach the feelings, the love, was there, as if it never left. I wanted to kiss her. Crash my lips down on hers and tell her how much she'd always meant to me. I leaned in, gently tucking a loose strand of hair behind her ear.

"Do you want to do something crazy?"

Lydia's eyes flitted shut and she nodded. I knew she was waiting for me to kiss her but now wasn't the time. I wanted her to remember everything about when we used to be together. The fun times. All the laughs. Because I felt that if she could remember, she wouldn't be able to leave. Not again. Reaching down underneath the end table, I grabbed a board game and shook it, causing the pieces to rattle.

Lydia opened her eyes and took in a deep breath before erupting into a fit of laughter.

"Scrabble?" She still laughed. "I remember we used to play this all the time."

I wiped away a tear that had fallen from her laughter, our face still inches apart.

"What do you say? Let me kick your butt like old times?" I smirked.

Lydia took a step back, and the fire in her eyes that always made its appearance when she meant business surfaced. Taking off her hoodie, she threw it on my couch.

"Oh, it's on." Smiling, I watched her set up the game, all while humming *Hey Ya* by The Outkast, one of the songs that we'd listened to when we were inseparable. She was coming back to me. Lydia Duncan was coming home.

Chapter Seven

Lydia

Ty's brows furrowed together, his eyes turning a deep shade of blue as he concentrated on the board in front of him. I'd just put the word Xerox down, which scored me nineteen points. We were neck and neck. Tied for first place.

"Z.E.P.H.Y.R. for..." Ty counted his points and I grumbled in front of him. He did this every time we played. Came out of the blue with a random word with letters that easily made him win. "Twenty-three points." Ty grinned at me, his dimples shining in his victory.

"Okay. But before we crown you the victor, define the word." I crossed my arms, my own smile flitting across my face, because I didn't even know what that word meant.

"It means a slight or gentle wind." Ty smirked. Putting up my finger, I snatched my cell phone out from next to me and searched for the word. I bypassed the messages from Lee and work, not wanting to bother with anyone from the outside world right now. When you were on Nantucket, even though it was part of Massachusetts, you couldn't help but feel like you were somehow separate. On a secluded island, just for yourself and those you cared about where no one could bother you and work didn't exist. Well, the fifteen messages from work and twenty emails let me know work really did exist and was starting to pile up.

"Wow. Every single time." I slammed my phone down and shook my head at his win.

Ty stood up and started dancing, doing some odd moves between the sprinkler and the Charleston.

"You're a child." I laughed as I stood up and started gathering the dishes from the table. We'd had popcorn and candy. Ty had come out with chocolate-covered peanuts, one of my favorite candies, and to the popcorn he'd added extra butter and salt. It had had just the right amount to clog your arteries enough to last a lifetime. All things I'd loved growing up. All things he'd never forgotten.

"Wow, it's really one a.m.?" Ty yawned and helped me bring the dishes to the kitchen. "I've got inventory tomorrow. Well, today."

I laughed. "How is it, owning your own store? Candy all day. I'm surprised you aren't a thousand pounds." I playfully whacked his stomach and was greeted with a solid mass of muscle.

A six-pack of solid muscle. Of course my childhood love would turn out to be a fit, muscley man who remembered how I liked my popcorn ten years later. The universe has forsaken me.

"Rock-hard abs." Ty smirked before starting to load the dishwasher. I rinsed the dishes and handed them to him. Oddly, it was all so domesticated and comfortable.

"So, the store?" I questioned again, as he was lost in his own thoughts as he loaded the dishes.

"Oh, sorry. Was just thinking." Ty shrugged as he took a bowl from my hands.

"About what?"

"How nice this was. Like old times. I missed this. I missed you." He closed the dishwasher and my wet hands hung limply at my sides, dripping small droplets of water on his floor. Ty and I were already close together but he closed the little gap that was between us before I could blink.

"Do you feel the same, Lyd? Tell me you missed me like I missed you." His breath kissed my lips and I was brought back to the first time his lips had ever touched mine.

Winter had settled in on the island, the cool breeze of the ocean replaced with a bitter wind that took your breath away when you stepped outside. Ty had insisted that we go snowshoeing. Dylan had refused and sat by the fire. I wished I'd stayed home with him. I couldn't feel my toes or my fingers.

"Ty, how much longer? I'm turning into an icicle," I whined.

Ty stopped and walked toward me, the shoes awkward as he tried to take bigger steps. I giggled at the sight of him, the big goggles he wore to protect his eyes and his gloves making him look more like a cartoon character than anything else.

"Let me see." Placing the goggles on top of his head and removing his gloves, he held out his hands and I placed my frozen hands in his. Slowly he took off my gloves before rubbing my hands together and breathing on them. The

friction of his hands, coupled with his breath, warmed me instantly. Ty always could. With just a look. Just a touch. He was my sun when the sky was gloomy. Ty was my smile when all I wanted to do was frown. He was my everything.

"Lydia, what if I told you that I love you?" Snow was falling, the large flakes peppering Ty's face with white. In this light, with the sun hitting the ground, the snow all around us, his eyes were so blue they stole my breath.

"I love you too." I smiled as he continued to rub my hands.

"No. Love you. Like I want to kiss you love you."

I took in a sharp breath, my sixteen-year-old mind trying to fathom what he was saying. I'd known that Ty and I were treading on relationship territory after the last few days , but I'd never thought he loved me. Not like that. His words warmed my frozen toes, and my nose that I knew was red and made me look like an odd version of a snowman, but I knew he didn't care. Ty Rue loved me.

I closed my eyes, snowflakes taking up residence against my eyelids. Then I felt it. Ty's lips gently touched mine.

As I opened my eyes, Ty gazed at me, his dark hair turned white. With a giggle, I brushed off his hair.

"I'd say I love you too, Ty Rue. Always have. Always will."

With a smile, Ty took my hand in his. The rest of the way back home, my body wasn't frozen, it was warm. As warm as a summer day on the beach with the sun radiating. Ty Rue was my warmth. He was perfection, and he loved me.

I hadn't realized it before, but ever since leaving Nantucket, I'd been cold. No man had ever made me feel like Ty had that day. I wanted to feel that way again. Sometimes it takes seeing those you love the most to realize how badly you missed them.

"I'm not sure if I missed you." I smirked as Ty's eyes narrowed and turned dangerously dark.

"I'll get you to say it if it kills you. I know you missed me."

I bit my bottom lip and took a step back, my body wanting so badly to be close to him again.

"I should get going. I've got to meet with the funeral home at noon and you have inventory."

Wiping my hands on the towel that hung from his cabinet, Ty never took his eyes off me. "You're right. I'll pick you up at six," he said.

"What? I'll be sleeping until eleven-forty-five. Rolling out of bed to throw on clothes before meeting the funeral director."

"You lost. I get to pick my prize. Don't you remember how the game's played?"

I groaned, remembering the week of lunches I'd had to make him and the laundry I'd had to do when he had won before.

"Six a.m.? That's in five hours!" I whined.

"Five and a half now." Ty laughed.

"You trying to kill me?" I stomped into the living room, putting on my hoodie and grabbing my phone.

Ty met me at the front door. I tried not to stare but I couldn't help it. Ty had grown into such a handsome man. He was taller than I remembered and I had to crane my neck to look up at him. I didn't mind the little crick in my neck because I loved looking at him.

"Not trying to kill you, Lyd. Just trying to make you remember." He leaned in and brushed a kiss to my cheek. It wasn't on my lips, but my God did it have the same effect. I closed my eyes and felt the softness of his lips against my skin, the sweetness that radiated all over my body and made me want to feel those lips as often as I could. I couldn't remember the last time I'd felt like this. Winning a case gave me a high, but Ty's lips on my skin were better than winning any case. Ty's lips were everything I had been missing.

"Goodnight, Ty." My voice was nothing more than a whisper.

"Night." Ty stood in the doorway, watching me walk to my mother's car, and waved as I drove away. Catching a glimpse of my reflection in the rear-view mirror, I couldn't help but notice the smile that was on my face. I hadn't smiled this big in years. Despite the death of my father, Ty made me smile just like he always had.

Ty didn't need to make me remember because I did. The memories, while they faded into the background of my chaotic, career-filled life, my childhood here on Nantucket, the happiness I felt, I pushed it all away.

Truth was, remembering was hard because I missed it all. Remembering made me long for who I was before. And that was difficult to balance. Work was easier in that way. I kept my head down, focused hard and was successful. Those memories? They hurt.

Fussing with the radio, I stopped at the station that played music that we'd grown up with, music Ty and Dylan had taught me to dance to. The music we'd blare in Ty's truck as we drove all around the island, causing the old people to tell our parents we were too loud and causing a disturbance. With the windows down and a smile on my face, I felt as if no matter what this week brought, with planning my father's funeral and grieving, Ty would try to find a way to make me smile.

Chapter Eight

Ty

Using my key, I let myself into the Duncans' home. It was six-ten and I had called Lydia a few times with no answer. *She never was a morning person.*

Dylan grumbled as he shuffled into the kitchen. His hair was crazy and matted against his head. He yawned and tripped over his own feet.

"Good morning," I said.

"Nothing good about mornings. I'd rather be asleep." Dylan opened the fridge, pulled out a carton of orange juice and drank it straight out of the carton.

"Don't let your mother see you doing that."

Dylan wiped his orange juice mustache off with the back of his hand.

"Why are you here this early?" Dylan held up his hand to stop me. "Wait, don't tell me. I don't want to know what you and my sister do behind closed doors."

I chuckled. "Want to help me wake her up? She lost at Scrabble last night and has to help me with inventory."

Dylan smirked and put the carton of orange juice away. Rubbing his hands together like he was about to get the greatest gift ever, he smiled.

"Let's do this."

With Dylan leading the way and me at his back, we tiptoed toward Lydia's room. Pearl came out of her bedroom and looked at us, shook her head, and headed into the kitchen.

"These kids never grow up," she mumbled.

Carefully, Dylan opened the door, inch by inch to make sure that it didn't make a sound. I glanced around for any booby traps. When we were younger, we'd made it a habit to try to wake one another up in the most creative ways—which had resulted in water buckets over doors, tape in doorways, anything we could think of to prank one another first thing in the morning.

Dylan and I each took a side of her bed and fought back our laughter at the sight of her. She was sprawled out, one leg hanging over the side of the bed. Her hair was wrapped crazily around her face, which was covered in a green mask.

With my fingers, I gave a one, two, three before Dylan and I both jumped on her.

"What the heck!" Lydia yelled as Dylan held her down and I tickled her.

"Stop! I have to pee," Lydia squealed.

Dylan pulled her by the legs straight off the bed. With a thud, she fell on her butt.

"You guys suck!" she huffed as she stood up.

"You're late." I tapped my watch.

"And molting." Dylan chuckled. "I've got to get ready to head into work for a few hours before we meet at the funeral home." Dylan leaned in and attempted to kiss Lydia on the cheek. "Yeah. No kiss for you." He patted her playfully on the shoulder.

Lydia stuck out her tongue.

"Real mature," Dylan said.

I threw myself down on her bed. Putting my arms behind my head and making myself comfortable, I watched her rifle through her bag,

"Says the man who just tickled me awake." Lydia shook her head, a smile flitting across her green face. "Give me ten minutes and I'll be ready."

Jumping off her bed, I sauntered toward the door, taking a second to look around her room. Nothing had changed. Our pictures still hung on the walls with heart-shaped thumbtacks, her stuffed animals still cluttered the floor where they must have fallen from the bed. It was like her room had been frozen in time, waiting for her to return.

"Take a whole hour. It'll take that long for you to chisel that goop off your face." I ducked as Lydia threw a stuffed bear at my head.

She stomped toward her bedroom door, her mask cracked from smiling earlier. With a slam, she shut the door.

I chuckled as I walked back to the kitchen, toward the smell of coffee and the laughter of my second family.

* * * *

"What are you kids up to today?" Pearl slid a cup of black coffee in front of me before returning to the pan of eggs she was scrambling. "Want some eggs?"

"No, thanks. Lydia is helping me with inventory for a bit."

Pearl smiled. "I'm glad. Her phone has been buzzing nonstop since she got here. I'm surprised she even has time to breathe."

"I've got time to breathe, Mom. In between winning cases and being a kick-butt lawyer." Lydia placed her purse and phone on the counter where I stood and headed to the fridge. Pulling out the carton of orange juice, she took a swig.

Like sister, like brother.

Pearl swatted her with a dishrag.

"I didn't raise you as a heathen. Use a glass!"

Lydia laughed and I joined her.

Lydia's phone buzzed on the counter and I caught a glimpse of an incoming message.

Lee: *Hope you're doing okay. I miss you.*

I snapped my eyes back up to Pearl and Lydia, who were chatting about the day's plans. A pit churned in my stomach, the black coffee not settling well. Did she have someone back in Boston? Lydia tilted her head back and laughed, and my heart clenched. I didn't want to come between her and her happiness, and if Lee was that for her, then so be it. But I wouldn't go down without a fight. I'd let her go before and I wouldn't make that mistake again, at least, not without her knowing how much I love her.

"Want a coffee for the road, sweetie?" Pearl stood on her tiptoes to reach the top cabinet and pulled down two travel mugs.

"Oh no. Ty's getting me Starbucks on the way to the shop." She winked at me.

"Am I now?" I raised my eyebrow and pushed myself away from the counter. Her phone buzzed again. Lydia sighed.

"This thing never stops." She frowned as she typed out a message. I wondered if she was texting Lee that she missed him too. Shaking my head, I tried to focus on what was in front of me, and that was her.

"Let's go. Don't want my chocolate melting out in the sun," I said.

Lydia shoved her phone in her bag.

"Mmmm. Melted chocolate is my favorite."

I smiled and nodded like what she was saying was something new to me. But it wasn't. I remembered everything she liked. You just can't forget the woman you love's favorite candy or food. How she isn't a morning person, but if you give her coffee she'll love you forever. Or how she's the world's most competitive Scrabble player but hasn't won a game. You simply don't just forget your one and only love.

* * * *

After grabbing Starbucks and Lydia professing her love to the nonfat caramel macchiato at least twenty times before we made it to the shop, we started inventory.

"I think I have a sugar high just from being in here so long. It smells like chocolate and peppermint and oranges. I smell *oranges.*" Lydia sat on the floor and crossed her legs as she opened the box in front of her.

"Oh, my God! Orange sticks. My favorite." She jumped up, clutching the candy to her chest.

"Take some." I laughed as I lined the shelves with the new taffy that had come in.

"You spoil me." She skipped over and kissed my cheek. I didn't expect it so I moved my face toward hers, our lips connecting briefly.

"I'm sorry." Lydia blushed and clutched the candy to her more tightly.

I smiled and tried to focus on stacking the shelves but who was I kidding? After our lips touching, even if by accident, I wanted more.

The door to the shop jingled and Greg, one of the staff, walked in. He was a good kid, had just graduated high school and was figuring out what to do with the rest of his life. I had been happy to offer him a job.

"Hey, boss," Greg said as he walked behind the counter.

"Greg Frisley, is that you!" Lydia bounced over to him. "When I saw you last you were this big." She motioned to her waist.

"I'm all grown up now," he laughed. "It's good to see you. I'm sorry about your dad." They hugged. Greg looked awkward, like he didn't know what to do with his hands. *Oh, to be eighteen again.*

"Thanks. So, how is it working for this guy?" She motioned to me with her hand.

"He's great. I get candy whenever I want it so I can't complain."

I chuckled. "All right, I'm heading out. If you need me for anything I've got my cell on."

"You got it!" Greg saluted before continuing to stock the shelves.

"Where are you going?" Lydia asked.

"It's almost noon. I'm going with you to the funeral home." I grabbed my jacket from the coat rack.

Tears welled up in Lydia's eyes. "You're coming with me?" Her voice cracked.

"Of course. I'll be with you every step of the way." Lydia reached out and took my hand in hers. We walked out of the store hand in hand.

A few locals stopped and looked at us, not trying to be discreet as they pointed and whispered. I think I even saw one person snap a photo with their phone.

"Everyone's going to be talking about us," I commented as we got into my truck.

"Let them talk," Lydia said as she stared out of the window.

I'd let them talk because I so badly wanted Lydia to be in my life permanently, and not as a friend but as the woman I would spend the rest of my life with.

Chapter Nine

Lydia

As I stepped into the funeral home, the squishy red carpet was too soft against my weak legs, which barely propelled me forward. The lights were dimmed, I assumed to meet the mood of those coming to talk about services for those they loved. They were too low and made me want to crawl out of my own skin. Everything about this place made me uneasy. Soothing music played in the background, making me hyperaware of my own emotions. It didn't soothe me, it put me on edge. Every sound caused goosebumps to form on my skin.

My mind, though, was numb. I guess that would be the best description. I was just going through the motions and half wanting to kick and scream like a child and exclaim the injustice of losing my father so quickly and unexpectedly.

Ty didn't say anything as we walked through the funeral home and to the back where the office was. I followed the subtle murmurs of voices, which I knew were my mother's and Dylan's. Their cars were already out front. My mother was always early. She always said if you weren't early, you were late. I glanced at the time on my phone, which had just turned twelve. I was right on time.

"Lydia. It's been forever. Look at you." Frank Littleton, the proprietor of Nantucket Funeral Services, stood up and hugged me. He was old enough to be my grandfather and to be honest, he'd always made me feel uncomfortable. given me the creeps. His back hunched a bit when he walked and his cane scraped against the floors, sounding like something out of a scary movie. But he was a nice guy and had never treated me and my family with anything but kindness.

Dylan, Ty and I used to peer into the funeral parlor windows to try to see the dead bodies. Creepy, I know, but there wasn't much to do around the island in the name of entertainment. So in the rare instance when someone died on the island, everyone talked about it and our childhood imaginations had always gotten the better of us.

"Hoist me up!" I ordered Dylan as we stood outside of the funeral home.

"You don't want to see a dead body," Dylan teased. "It'll be all wrinkly and gross." Dylan made a face like he was going to vomit.

"Come on! Hoist me up!" I clawed at the window, not yet tall enough to see.

"Fine." Dylan groused as he made a little step with his knee. Ty stood watch so we wouldn't get caught.

I stood on Dylan's knee and he moaned under the pressure of my weight.

"Lay off the candy, will you?" he chuckled.

"Shut up!" I swatted at him. I gasped when I saw Mr. Abbott. He wasn't wrinkly and didn't have an eyeball missing or green, oozing skin. He looked like himself. Like the man who would give us hard candy when we walked by his house after school. Mrs. Abbott would yell at him and tell him he was ruining our dinner but he'd wink and give us a few extra just out of spite.

"Someone's coming!" Ty called out.

Dylan dropped me to the ground. "Run! Meet you at home." Dylan took off running.

"Come on." Ty took my hand in his as we ran through the small, wooded area toward my house.

"My own brother left me," I huffed as we were finally out of the woods and walking down the street.

"It's okay. I'll never leave you, Lyd."

I hadn't fully understood Ty's words that night, but he'd stayed true to them even a decade later when I'd left him to pursue my own dream. If that wasn't true love, I don't know what was. And now I felt his hand on the small of my back and I knew I could do anything with him by my side. Beyond my job, becoming partner, none of that seemed matter, because what I needed suddenly shifted to the island that had once been my home.

"It's good to see you again, Mr. Littleton."

"Here, have a seat." Dylan stood up and pulled out the chair for me to sit down.

"Thanks." I slid in, my mother immediately taking my hand in hers.

"Okay. Well, I wish we were meeting under different circumstances but alas, we are here to discuss the end-of-life services for William."

Mom sniffed and dabbed her eyes. I fought back an eyeroll. *"End of life."* It was death. Final and absolute. This wasn't a walk on the beach that my father had decided on or a birthday party we needed to plan, this was my father's life being reduced to a cremation and a few spoken words.

"I'll be taking care of the cremation tomorrow. You can come…" His voice drifted out as I gazed out of the window. It was a beautiful fall day. The sun was shining, the birds chirping noisily outside the window. I focused on the clock that ticked as each second drifted by. My shoulders were squeezed and I looked back at Ty, who stood over me, gripping me softly and bringing me back to the present. I placed my hand on the top of his, thankful that he'd come.

"I'd like to see him," I blurted out. All eyes were on me. I wasn't even sure what point of the conversation I'd interrupted as I'd barely been listening. I needed to see my father one last time before his body was no longer here.

"Honey, I'm not sure that's a good idea." Mom glanced over at Dylan and Ty.

"I need to. For closure."

Ty squeezed my shoulders again and Mr. Littleton cleared his throat.

"That can be arranged. After we finish up here I can take you back."

"Thank you. I'd appreciate that."

My mother sobbed again, as if the thought of me seeing my father one last time was too much for her to bear. I didn't know what to expect, and this very well could be a bad idea, but I needed to do this. To say goodbye.

* * * *

They say a girl's father is the first man she ever loves. It's true. I remember staring at my father in awe when he'd leave for work in his police uniform, his gun clipped to his side. He was my real-life superhero. He'd ruffle my hair and kiss my forehead, no matter how old I got, and tell me to make good choices. I watched him love my mother with all of himself, treating her with nothing but respect and kindness. Every morning he'd kiss her on the lips, causing my aging mother to giggle like a schoolgirl. When he'd come home, no matter how late or how exhausting his day had been, he'd sit and ask my mother about her day and listen. I mean really listen to her and engage in conversation. My father taught me how a man should treat a woman and my expectations had been set incredibly high because I wanted what he and my mother had. Not just a romantic love, but a friendship. A love so deep that the thought of your significant other not being happy or comfortable made you unhappy and uncomfortable. A connection. A soulmate.

I followed Mr. Littleton to the back of the funeral home, the atmosphere getting colder by the second. Everyone had offered to come with me but I needed to do this alone.

Mr. Littleton stopped in front of a gurney with a white sheet covering my father's body.

He pulled the sheet back, stopping at the base of my father's neck.

With a shaky hand, Mr. Littleton gripped my shoulder. "I'll give you a few minutes to say goodbye."

I listened as he walked away and heard the door latch before I allowed myself to really look at my father. He looked peaceful, almost as if he were asleep. Brushing back his salt-and-pepper hair, I let my tears fall. I felt safe next to him, that no one could judge me in this moment that I was sharing with my father. Sobs took over my body, my shoulders shaking under their force. My father was gone. He'd never walk me down the aisle or hold his grandchildren. There'd be so much he'd miss and that broke my heart, sending it shattering into little pieces. I'd always thought that once I settled down and had kids I'd bring them to the island and they'd run down the beach with my father. He'd put them on his shoulders like he used to do with Dylan and me and tell them all about the history of the island. The place he loved so much. There'd be none of that now. It was all up to me and that scared me. I was married to my job and, while I wanted a family of my own, I knew it would be hard to make partner and be the mother I wanted to be. I knew plenty of working mothers who were great and balanced things well. But I wasn't sure I could do it.

"I'm going to miss you." I sniffed. "I wish I'd come home more. That I didn't stay away so long." I knew if he were alive right now he'd tell me to work hard and don't worry about him. He'd pushed me to succeed, not in an overbearing way, but my dreams had been his. But was it all worth it? The late nights and study sessions, not eating for days and hustling from case to case? If feeling like I'd missed out on a part of my life that had once meant so much to me was the price, I didn't know if I wanted to continue to pay it. Not anymore. And that was tough to comprehend when my entire life had been structured around becoming a lawyer and moving to Boston.

I could have it all, right?

Pulling the sheet back over my father's face and taking a deep breath, I headed back to my family.

"I love you, Dad," I said out loud as I shut the door behind me.

Ty stood on the other side, holding up the wall with his muscular frame. He was everything my father had been. A good man who loved with his whole heart and never let go, even when he should have. Our eyes met and everything in my mind stilled. My feet, as if they knew what my heart and mind wanted, brought me to the man that I had fallen in love with ten years ago. I fell into his arms, which wrapped around me like they had been waiting for me all this time. As he rubbed my back and whispered sweet words into my ear, I rested my head against Ty's chest and listened to his breathing. I never wanted him to let me go because if this was how I could feel every day of my life, like I was slowly breaking and being put back together again, more whole and beautiful than before, I wanted this, to feel whole again.

Chapter Ten

Ty

I walked into the Duncans' house after school with Dylan close on my heels. As I slung my bag on Dylan's bed, I heard Lydia's muffled whimpers.

"What's wrong with her?" I asked Dylan.

"No idea. Probably girl stuff." Dylan powered on his computer and made no movements to see what was wrong with his sister.

"I'm going to make sure she's okay."

"All right. Take some chocolate with you just in case. Throw it at her and back away slowly if she starts to growl." He chuckled. At seventeen years old I probably shouldn't have cared so much about my best friend's fifteen-year-old sister, but there was something about her that made me want to protect her. Not in a brotherly way, in a gushy way that made me all sorts of confused.

"Lyd?" I gently knocked on the door and opened it, catching sight of her huddled on her bed, her eyes red-rimmed and her face splotchy.

"What's wrong?" I sat down on her bed.

"Go away, Ty, I don't want to be made fun of right now." She lay down on the bed and put the pillow over her face.

"I'm not going to make fun of you. Tell me what happened." I removed the pillow and she groaned.

I poked her ribs for a few minutes before she finally gave up.

"It was Eric, okay! He broke up with me and called me boring because I read my law books all the time. Am I that boring?" Lydia sat up and tucked her legs underneath her. "Tell me the truth, I can take it. Geri says I'm not but she's my best friend." She squared her shoulders, clearly waiting for whatever truth I was about to give her. Geri had moved to the island a year ago with her mother, who was an artist. She and Lydia had become good friends almost immediately.

I grunted "Eric Grady is nothing but a stupid jock." Eric was a junior like me and loved the younger girls because they were like putty in his hands. I'd nearly broken his face when I'd heard he was dating Lydia.

"Stop being stereotypical. He's not stupid. He just struggles in school." I caught a hint of a smile whisk across Lydia's face.

"I betcha he wouldn't know a law book if it hit him in the face." That got a giggle out of Lydia.

"You didn't answer my question. Am I boring?"

I thought of all the times that we had snuck out of the house and gone to the beach after dusk. The few times we'd snuck to the funeral home to scope out what was going on. Sure, she'd bring a book with her sometimes, but she wasn't boring. Not in the least.

"You're you. You carry a book with you wherever you go. Which is why your right arm is more muscular than the left." I squeezed it. "But seriously, if he can't see how amazing you are then it's his loss. I told you Eric was a loser."

Lydia lay back on her bed and looked at her phone.

"Geri says you're right and I should listen to you," Lydia said.

"Is that so? Now you listen to me because Geri said so?"

Lydia nodded. "Best friend rule. And she said you're cute." Lydia blushed.

"Do you think I'm cute?"

Lydia scrunched up her nose. "No way."

"Ouch." I put my hand over my heart.

"I think you're the hottest boy ever." Lydia jumped off her bed and looked at herself in the mirror.

"Want to go pick up Geri and get some ice cream?" Lydia asked, as if she hadn't just called me hot. "What? I'm sure you've been called hot before." She threw a pillow at my head. I caught it with my hand.

"Not by anyone that matters."

Lydia tilted her head to the side and studied me before letting out a sigh. "Come on, hot stuff. Let's cool down before I profess my love to you," Lydia joked as she held out her hand to help me off the bed.

In that moment, I'd fallen for my best friend's little sister.

As we pulled up to her parents' house, Lydia turned toward me and smiled. I realized that since that day she'd called me hot, no woman had ever come close to her. Sure, I'd dated since she left ten years ago, but no one was Lydia Duncan and no one ever would be. I'd stopped trying to date after my last relationship. The woman had said she didn't like the beach. I mean, who lives on an island surrounded by water and hates the beach? She'd moved off the island a few months later. I was sure I'd had something to do with that.

"Thanks for today. It was actually pretty fun to hang out at your store and get to be around candy all morning. You weren't so bad to hang out with either," Lydia teased.

"Any time you want to provide me with free labor, I'm all for it."

Lydia let out a small laugh, tucking her hair behind her ear. "And for coming with me to the funeral home. I'm not sure I would have managed to get through it without you."

"Stop saying thank you for everything, Lyd. I'm here. I'm your friend. I'm not going anywhere."

"Do you want to go for a drink later? I have to have dinner with my mom and some of our family that came over from the mainland but I'd love to buy you a drink or two. Catch up some more?" I could tell she was nervous because she fidgeted with the hem of her shirt.

"Justin's bar work? Around eight-thirty?" I tried to be as relaxed as possible, but everything in me was screaming that this was exactly what I had hoped. I wanted to spend as much time with Lydia as possible and this was my opportunity, something she had initiated.

"That's great. I'll meet you there."

I watched her walk to the door and make it safely inside before I pulled away and drove toward How Sweet It Is. I hadn't planned on going back today, but I needed a distraction until eight-thirty.

* * * *

I ordered two beers and waited at a table for Lydia. Justin stood at the bar, talking with a few locals who were in for a quick drink before going home for the night.

The door flew open and my mouth hung agape. Lydia wore a tight sweater dress the color of caramel, her hair loose around her face. Next to her was Geri, who had been her best friend in high school. Geri was taller than Lydia by a few inches, and looked very much the artist that she had become. Her hair was a perfect rainbow, and tattoos were visible all over her body.

"Geri!" I stood up, bringing her in for a hug. "Hell, it's been forever. How are you?"

"I'm great. Aren't you still the cutest thing?" Geri stepped back and looked at me, shaking her head. "Shame Lydia here claimed you before I had a chance."

Lydia blushed and sat down at our table.

"What brings you back to the island?"

"I heard about Mr. Duncan and wanted to be here for Lydia. He was like a father to us all." She went to sit down but her eyes snapped to the bar. "Who is that hunk of man over there?" She pointed to Justin, who looked at me with wide eyes. He'd clearly heard what she said.

"That's Justin."

"Justin. I love that name. I'll be back." With a flick of her hand, Geri left and sidled up to the bar and to Justin. I gave him a thumbs-up.

"Man, that's so nice of her to come here," I commented as I sat down.

"It is. Such a nice surprise to have her at dinner. Dylan arranged the whole thing. Go figure. Lydia shrugged and I made a mental note to ask Dylan about Geri later.

We both looked over at the bar as Justin laughed.

"I haven't heard him laugh like that in a while."

"Geri has that way about her. Her free spirit is infectious," Lydia said with a smile.

We clicked beer bottles in agreement before I got lost in my own mind. So many people from our younger years were here again. Albeit not under the best circumstances. But it was nice to see everyone again. It also made me realize all the things I wanted to know about Lydia.

"Penny for your thoughts?" I asked as Lydia twirled her beer around in her hands like it was fine wine.

"Just thinking of all the things I want to ask you. No idea where to start. Ten years is a long time."

"Good thing we can make up for it."

The way she said *time* made goosebumps travel all over my body. Did we have time? I knew that in just a week or so she'd be on that boat and back to a life that didn't include me when I so badly wanted it to.

"Who's Lee?" I blurted out.

Real smooth, Ty.

Lydia choked on her drink. Sitting back in her chair, she grinned.

"Are you snooping on me, Mr. Rue?"

"No. Well. Yes. I mean, kinda?" I laughed awkwardly. "I saw a message on your phone and he said he missed you. Just curious if you found the One, I guess?"

Lydia polished off her beer in long gulps before answering.

"I went to law school with Lee. We've been friends for a few years and he told me when he dropped me off at the boat to come here that he had feelings for me. I knew it deep down but hearing it him say it..." She picked at the label on the beer bottle.

I waited for her to finish her sentence but nothing else came.

"So, are you going to tell him that you just want to be friends or that you have feelings for him too?" I held my breath.

"I think deep down he knows that we will never be more than friends. But yeah, I'm going to tell him. What about you? Any future Mrs. Rue lined up?"

I let out my breath. "That depends."

"On what?" Lydia asked.

I was feeling mighty brave in the moment and went with it. What did I have to lose? "On her." I kept my eyes pinned on Lydia's as she made a slight O shape with her mouth. I had lost Lydia once and I didn't know if I could handle seeing her walk away again. At this point, I had to fight. Show her all she had missed. Where she'd come from. Who she'd used to be before she got wrapped up in the corporate world and fast-paced city life.

I had to remind her of when things were simpler. Just two kids in love, dreaming of what could be.

"Guys! Let's dance." Geri pulled me off the chair and Justin grabbed Lydia. The bar was empty and the country music that Justin insisted be played twenty-four-seven had been turned up.

Geri and Lydia started moving chairs and tables to make a makeshift dance floor as Justin slapped my shoulder.

"Where did she come from?" Justin motioned to Geri, her wild-colored hair highlighted by the lights.

"New York City. She moved there after high school to do artist stuff."

"Ah. Well, I want one of her." Smiling, Justin wrapped his arms around Geri's waist before twirling her around.

Lydia motioned to me with her finger, and I was hypnotized as she moved her hips. She snaked her arms around my neck and we slowed danced and gazed into each other's eyes.

"This music sucks." She scrunched her nose.

Clearing my throat, I started singing *How Sweet It Is To Be Loved By You*.

Lydia laughed, and Geri and Justin made cat-meowing-in pain noises. I was no singer.

"My favorite song," Lydia whispered once everyone had settled down. Resting her head on my chest, she hummed, not caring that other music played in the background. I felt the vibrations of her sweet voice against me and gently caressed her hair.

A few people staggered in, and Justin and Geri left the dance floor. I looked up as Geri sat at the bar as Justin served drinks. She winked at me, holding up her drink in a silent toast.

Lydia and I didn't move. We stayed in each other's arms swaying side to side to a song that only we could hear. The song that was ours and I knew that no matter what happened between us, it always would be.

Chapter Eleven

Lydia

Geri lay next to me in my bed, her hair balancing precariously on the top of her head. Any sudden movement would send it cascading down. The color had turned heads when we walked home tonight, but I loved her spunk. We couldn't be more different. Me with my perfectly pressed dress suits and her with her free-flowing skirts and funky hair.

"I think I'm in love." Geri huffed and texted on her phone. "Justin is not like any of the men in New York."

I balanced my computer on my lap and tried to get through the emails that had piled up. I'd managed to get all my contracts done. I don't know how but I had. My boss, Franklin, was pleased with me, so there was that I guess. Oddly, where before that would have made me jump for joy, now it didn't. I deleted his email and snapped my laptop shut.

"You just met him." I snuggled into the blankets and turned toward Geri.

"Not everyone can be childhood sweethearts and gaze into each other's eyes as they dance to music in their heads." She made a dramatic batting movement with her eyelashes.

"Oh please." I repositioned myself onto my back and stared at the ceiling, which had glow-in-the-dark stickers on it. Some were shaped like stars, others like various planets.

"Remember when we used to go stargazing in high school?" Geri smiled as she looked up at the ceiling.

"I do. That's when I thought I wanted to marry your brother."

I laughed and closed my eyes, remembering the times when we were carefree and just living for the day.

"I think Geri has a crush on Dylan." Ty and I looked over as Geri swatted Dylan playfully on the arm. He didn't seem to mind the extra attention and reached out and tugged on the ends of her hair.

"Geri has a crush on everyone." I shrugged. It was true. Geri liked boys. Any boy. She didn't discriminate. She claimed that she wouldn't know when she'd found the One unless she'd dated as many people as she could. We were fifteen. I had no desire to find my happily ever after until I was at least thirty. That was my plan. Go to college, focus on my studies then get married and have a few kids at thirty. I figured that was a good age.

"The moon's so bright tonight," Ty said as I gazed up.

"It is. It's beautiful."

"Like you."

I looked over at him, and a small smile spread across his face.

"Can I take you on a date?"

"A date? Me?" My brain got all fuzzy and I couldn't make sense of what he was asking. Ty Rue wanted to take me out?

"Yeah, you." He nudged me with his shoulder. "Because I like you. We can go anywhere you want."

My heart fluttered and I gazed at Ty, the light of the moon illuminating the features of his face. He was handsome, by far the best-looking boy at school. Dylan was a close second, but he was my brother and I would never admit that to his face. Girls were always jealous that Ty hung out with me and made comments sometimes that it was out of pity and because of me being Dylan's little sister.

"Why me?" I had to know why.

"You're interesting. I love talking to you about law, books and everything." He laughed. "You've grown into one of my best friends. I have Dylan, but we don't talk about the things you and I do. You're so beautiful but you don't even know it. You're different than all the other girls who flaunt their big boobs and slather on makeup. You're beautiful because you have a good heart and soul."

I struggled to find my words. Ty really did like me.

"I guess a date wouldn't hurt. I want ice cream. Double scoops." I smirked and continued to stare at the moon.

"Double-scooped ice cream. Got it. Thanks for the chance. I won't let you down." Ty slipped his hand in mine.

It wasn't him letting me down that I worried about, it was me. I'd never dated a boy like Ty before, and the one time I'd tried with Eric, he'd thought I was boring. But with Ty, I couldn't help but feel like what we had was different. It was real. As real as a fifteen-year-old relationship could be. Ty squeezed my hand.

Okay, maybe what we had was more.

"Do you ever wish we could go back to those times when we were young and just living our lives for ourselves?" I asked, holding onto the memory.

"Sometimes. Being an adult isn't all I expected it to be," Geri said. "I always wanted to be older. Be an adult and make all my own choices. But now that I have. It's for the birds." She sighed.

Geri seemed to be struggling with something, but I didn't want to pry. There was much about Geri that no one even knew. She was an artist, doing what, she never shared but you could tell by the tattoos that peppered her body, her funky hair and unique clothes, she lived for art in all its forms. She'd always lived to the beat of her own drum, and it just made sense, and no one questioned her. But something had changed. I just didn't know what.

But she was one of my oldest friends and whenever she was ready to share what she was struggling with, I'd be there.

"Amen to that. I wanted so bad to be a lawyer and now that I am, it's all I have time for. Sometimes I want more. To settle down, get married and have kids. I waited and focused on my career and now my dad won't be here to see me actually living. I never thought of that possibility and the reality hurts." Tears burned my eyes.

"Oh, sweetie. We're only twenty-eight. We have time. Don't feel bad for focusing on your dream."

The tears streamed down my face. "I'm not sure that my dream is what I want anymore. God, how crazy does that sound? I love being a lawyer, but I don't want that to be all that I am, you know?"

"Absolutely. It's okay to want to be loved and to want to find that happiness. Even though I think you already have." She made a coughing motion and said Ty's name.

"Stop! Ty and I are complicated," I muttered.

"Only as complicated as you make it. You two need to just rip the Band-Aid off already and tell each other how you feel. It's like a tennis match watching you both go back and forth."

"I live in Boston and he has his business here," I said out loud, like it would make the feelings that overcame me every time I was near Ty go away.

"His business that he named after your song. Don't act like everyone doesn't know that. He never stopped loving you, Lydia. How you don't wrap yourself around his legs and never let him go is beyond me." Geri shrugged.

Sighing, I leaned over and turned off the light, and the stars and planets on the ceiling began to glow. Geri didn't know what it was like to be torn between two worlds. I had my life in Boston that had been fine for the past decade until I came home. Now I couldn't deny the draw I had to the one place I hadn't been able to get away from fast enough.

Geri smiled as her phone buzzed. "Now Justin... I may have not known him since I was in diapers, but I know a good soul. I can feel his pain, but underneath that is a man who I know is nothing short of amazing."

I didn't say anything in response to Geri's comment about Justin. I fell asleep to the sound of her texting, a few of her giggles joining in and forming the perfect lullaby.

Chapter Twelve

Ty

It was Thursday, my favorite day of the week. I know most people lived for Fridays, when the weekend was right around the corner, but for me, Thursdays were Candy and Story Time at How Sweet It Is. The preschool class came over to the store and enjoyed a story and a treat.

I walked into the small library like I did every Thursday. Louise, the librarian, held up a book for me.

I handed her a coffee and a bag of peppermints, our weekly trade off.

"I picked a good one for you this week." She smiled, her teeth stained with red lipstick.

"*Chicka Chicka Boom Boom*. Can't say I ever read it, but it looks good." I flipped through the colorful pages.

"Oh, those little ones will love it, trust me!" She laughed and returned to the book cart.

"I'll see you next week, Louise!" I called out. She waved as she talked to herself. Or the books. She loved books more than anyone I knew.

I made my way back to the store and set up the mats for the kids before getting together the snack for today. I went with something easy, bite-size candy in various fun shapes and flavors.

The door opened just as I finished putting out the food, the laughter of the kids carrying in.

"Mr. Ty!" they squealed before tackling my legs. I laughed as I greeted each one as the teachers tried to settle them down.

"Not sure they need sugar today," Lindsay, one of the preschool teachers, said.

"I wouldn't be cool Mr. Ty if I didn't give them candy."

She rolled her eyes and tried to get a few of them to sit down.

"All right, my friends, who's ready for a story!"

"Yay!" They all squealed and took their seats. I shrugged as Lindsay looked at me like I was the child whisperer.

"Today's story is *Chicka Chicka Boom Boom.*" I sat on the chair in front of them and showed the cover.

I started reading, getting lost in the different voices that I read in to keep them all entertained. The door dinged and I glanced up as Lydia stumbled in.

"I'm sorry," she muttered as she took in all the kids. A few of them looked at her but quickly diverted their attention back to me.

"It's okay. Stay." I motioned for her to sit down. She smiled before nodding and trying to find a free spot. She joined the kids on the floor, sitting cross-legged.

"You won't be sorry. He's a good storyteller," Jack, one of the little boys, said. Lydia smiled and gave me her full attention. I didn't hold back. My voices were spot-on and Lydia was laughing right along with the kids. I even added a few faces in to really get them going.

I finished reading and closed the book.

"Okay, who has questions about the story?" I asked. "Yes, Mary." I pointed to the cute little girl in pigtails.

"Who's she?" Mary pointed to Lydia.

"Well, that's a good question." I motioned for Lydia to stand up. She blushed but stood up and waved.

"Hi. I'm Lydia and I grew up on Nantucket."

Mary looked between us, her interest clearly piqued.

"Why'd you leave?" she asked.

"I went to college in Boston and became a lawyer." Our eyes met and the unspoken words hung between us. She should have stayed. I should have asked her to. Or better yet, I should have gone with her. Even if for a bit, to show her that I was serious about our relationship.

Mary nodded as if she knew what Lydia was talking about.

"You're pretty," Jack interrupted.

"All right there, Casanova. How about you start the line at the beginning of the table for snack?"

Jack clapped before jumping up, the rest of the kids rushing behind him.

"Hi." I smiled at Lydia. "Welcome to Thursday Story Time with my ten most favorite people."

Lydia looked back at them, almost a hint of sadness present in her eyes. "They are so cute. And totally smitten with you."

"I give them candy every week. What's not to love?"

Lydia laughed. "You always knew the way to a girl's heart."

"I do recall yours being hard to capture."

Lydia fake gasped. "Me? Never."

"Mr. Ty?" I looked down as my pant leg was tugged by Jack. "Will you and the pretty lady sit with me?"

Lydia smiled and kneeled so she was eye level with him. "We'd love to sit with you. Lead the way." She took his little hand in hers, and I followed behind them to the mats.

I watched as Lydia played with the kids and sang songs, clapping along excitedly like this was the most fun she'd had in years. She glanced up at me and smiled, and I sucked in a sharp breath. I had never seen her more beautiful. My mind filled with what ifs. Did she want kids of her own? She had to. She was a natural mother. The thought of our children running through the shop warmed me. I'd ply them with candy and she'd scold me because it was before dinner. Then I'd kiss her, she'd sigh and forget all about it. Because we were in love and nothing else mattered. Not candy before dinner or the past that separated us. Just our future together.

Each kid hugged Lydia and me, eagerly asking whether she would be here next week for story time. I knew she wouldn't be, but didn't have the heart to tell them.

"I'm sorry for just barging in. I didn't know you did this reading group. That was amazing. Their little faces." Lydia laughed as she helped me pick up the mats.

"That's okay. I think you're their new favorite now."

"No one is as cool as the guy with the candy." She winked.

"What made you drop by? Not that I minded at all."

Lydia stopped cleaning and her shoulders slumped. "Tomorrow's my dad's memorial service. Dylan, Mom and I decided to have it on the beach and then have dinner at the restaurant down by the water. We rented out the banquet room. Tons of people have already trickled in. My house is full. I'm just so overwhelmed I had to get away."

"Where are Dylan and Geri? Isn't she staying with you?" I grabbed the trash can and swiped all the leftover candy into it.

"Dylan's working tonight to get his mind off things and Geri is with Justin."

I raised my eyebrows.

"Don't ask. Apparently, it's love." Lydia laughed and rolled her eyes.

"Stay with me tonight." The words were out of my mouth before I thought better of it.

"What?" Lydia brought her hand to her neck like what I said was alarming.

"Not like that." I felt my face heat. "We can watch movies. I'll cook or we can order out. It'll be fun. Like old times. And it'll leave a bed open for someone at your house."

I could see the wheels turning in Lydia's mind. She bit her bottom lip before checking her phone.

"A free bed would help ease my mom's mind." She nodded. "Okay. Would you be able to pick me up? I have a few things to do to get ready for tomorrow but my mom needs the car tonight."

"Absolutely. I close at six. I'll be there shortly after."

"That sounds perfect." With a smile, Lydia went back to stacking the mats.

Tomorrow would be a difficult day for us all, as we laid her father to rest. He had been a pillar in the community and loved by so many. Everyone knew he'd loved Lydia with his whole heart, wanting only the best for her. I smiled fondly, remembering the day I'd asked him if I could date Lydia.

"Son, you're a good kid. All I ask is that you marry her one day."

"Sir?" I shoved my hands in my pockets. I was seventeen. While I wanted to date Lydia, marriage hadn't crossed my mind.

"I won't be around forever and I want her taken care of. Can you do that for me?"

"I'll always take care of her." I puffed out my chest proudly.

He nodded and pushed up his glasses, which were balancing on his nose.

"Good. You're young. I know you think I'm crazy but you two have something that I haven't seen since Pearl and me. A once-in-a-lifetime kind of love. Can't promise it'll be easy, but it'll be worth it.

"Yes, sir."

"Ty."

"Yes?"

"I've changed your diapers and seen you streak naked down the street. I think we're way past sir, don't you?"

"Okay, Mr. Duncan."

Lydia's father laughed and shook his head.

"Can't be mad at you for being proper. Now go ask my daughter out before she decides to date Eric again. Darn fool."

I'd skipped out of their house that day, with Lydia's father's blessing to date her. We'd gazed at the stars that night, and I'd asked her out. Thankfully she'd said yes, and everything else had seemed to fall into place — until it hadn't. William had looked at me the day she'd left for college and reminded me that it wouldn't be easy, but it would be worth it. I hadn't wanted to hear that then because I had been bitter and broken that she'd left me behind. Now, I just hated myself for letting her go.

Chapter Thirteen

Lydia

My mind was going a thousand miles a minute. I went and made sure everything was all set for the memorial service tomorrow. The restaurant was paid, the food picked out and I found a dress that didn't look like I was walking into the courtroom. I didn't want to be in a suit. That wasn't how my father remembered me. Catching a glimpse of myself in the window of a store, I looked at my jeans and T-shirt. This was how he remembered me. This was how I remembered myself. No tailored suits and tight buns that made me look like an angry ballerina. Not worried about making partner and letting life pass me by. I'd always cared about my grades and being a lawyer, but what was once a passion had quickly taken over my life. When I was a child, I'd still made time to live. To fall in love. None of that was a part of my life in Boston. Just being a lawyer and climbing that ladder all the way to the top.

My cell phone buzzed. As if knowing what I was thinking, the office was calling.

"This is Lydia." I tried to balance my bags on my arms and hold the phone against my ear. I may have gone overboard at the stores. I had forgotten how many cute little shops were on the island.

"I'm so sorry to bother you but Franklin told me to call you and he scares me so..." Abi rattled on and on.

"Abi, breathe. It's okay. I was just out doing a bit of shopping. What's up? I handed in all my contracts and all my loose ends are tied up. Did I miss something? I was pretty sure I hadn't forgotten anything.

"Yeah. About that. Franklin needs you back Monday."

I stopped in the middle of the sidewalk. A few people walking their dogs moved around me and I smiled in apology.

"My father's memorial service is tomorrow. Franklin granted me two weeks off. Not one." I ground my teeth together. I'd have to say goodbye to my father and have only the weekend with my family before returning to work? That wasn't what I'd agreed to.

"Something came up in court I guess and they need you there first thing Monday morning. You know if it wasn't important, he wouldn't demand it."

Demand. There it was. *Demanding* that I say goodbye to my father and hurry back because they needed me. Not my family, who hadn't seen me in years because I gave every waking second to Franklin and Collins. Not to mention there were other attorneys who could fill in for me. But I knew this was likely a test to see how badly I wanted partner.

"I'll come for court Monday but I'm coming back right after and spending the rest of the week with my family. Tell him that." My words came out harsh and I cringed. "Abi, I'm sorry, this isn't your fault. Don't worry about it. I'll send him an email and let him know I'll come back for court but I will be keeping the rest of my days off."

"Whew. Thank goodness, because he gets red in the face and looks like his head is going to pop off when I talk to him. I think I annoy him. Anyways, I miss you and this office stinks without you."

I smiled and breathed in, my nerves settling down.

"I miss you too. I'll see you Monday then."

"Bye-bye, and I hope everything goes well tomorrow with the memorial. Know I've been thinking about you."

"Thank you, that means a lot." Abi may be my secretary, but we had formed a solid friendship over the years. We'd shared many meals over paperwork and late-night conferences.

We ended the call and I replied to a few messages that Lee had sent. He had consistently checked in on me and I hadn't been too good about responding. I needed to spend as much time as possible focused on my family and healing. I didn't want to lead Lee on either, and if I replied too quickly, or too much, I feared that I would. I didn't want to tell him over text that we could never be anything more than friends. I figured that was a conversation better left for in person.

Making my way back home, I unpacked all my bags, threw clothes into an overnight bag, and was ready by the time Ty texted me.

Balancing my overnight bag in one hand and holding my dress on a hanger high above my head, I tried to quickly leave my bedroom.

"Use protection!" Dylan yelled after me as I headed out of the house.

"Are you moving in?" Ty quirked his eyebrow as he took the bag from my hand. His cheeks heated at Dylan's words but we both pretended that we didn't hear them. That's how everything has been these past few days. It was best to just ignore the feelings, and comments that others made. *I think.*

"Haha. Funny. I needed to make sure I have everything."

He groaned dramatically when he lifted the bag into the back of his truck. It really wasn't that heavy. I rubbed my arm where a red welt was forming from where the bag had been. Okay, maybe it was.

"Everything meaning you're prepared for a zombie apocalypse?"

"Full of jokes tonight, aren't you?" I clicked my seatbelt and tried to find a good radio station.

"Channeling my inner Rick Grimes."

"Who the heck is that?"

"Oh, don't tell me you've never seen *The Walking Dead*?" He stopped at the end of the driveway and stared at me, his mouth hanging open.

"Um, No." I shrugged. "I work twenty-four-seven. And when I'm not working I'm thinking about work."

"Dear God. We are so binge watching that tonight. It's settled."

"It sounds gory and like it's going to give me nightmares."

Ty smiled. "Gory doesn't even begin to describe it. Chomp, Chomp." He pretended he was chewing on my arm.

I squealed.

"Sorry, I'm a little hungry." Ty winked before he started driving again.

"Hey, isn't your house that way?" I pointed to a street that he passed by.

"Yes, it is. How observant of you." He stared straight ahead.

"Where are we going?"

He chuckled. "So, nosey. Sit back and relax. It's a surprise."

"I hate surprises," I mumbled and crossed my arms across my chest.

"I know, but sometimes you have to let go and just live." Ty's eyes sparkled as he said those words and I shivered. He's always had his way of knowing what I needed even without me having to say it. Even through the years, Ty remained my very best friend.

* * * *

We pulled up to a small cottage and I hopped out of the truck and stretched. It hadn't been a long ride, no drive was on Nantucket, but I wanted to feel the salt air all over my body. I heard the waves close by and wanted so badly to feel my toes in the sand.

"Come on." Ty took my hand, my bag hanging on his arm. We walked into the cottage and Ty placed my bag on the couch. "Close your eyes, Lyd."

Sighing, I let my mind still and closed my eyes. As we walked, I heard a door open, and listened to Ty's instructions.

"I'm going to take your shoes off." Balancing my hands on shoulder, I kept my eyes shut as he fumbled with my shoes. I giggled as he muttered obscenities under his breath.

"Okay, step down."

I did as he'd said and felt my toes hit the cool sand. We walked for a few minutes more before he stopped and pulled his hand out of mine.

"Open."

Slowly, I let my eyes flutter open. I gasped, and tears fill my eyes. On the beach, with the waves crashing in the background, was a table set for two, with candles and food out. The food was covered so I didn't know what it was but it didn't matter. This was the most romantic thing anyone had ever done for me.

Ty pulled out my chair. I was speechless. The fact that Ty had gone to this extent for me left me weak in the knees. Reaching out, I steadied myself against the table. This wasn't just a friendly gesture. This was thought out, romantic. Everything about this screamed love and compassion—things I never thought I'd have again. Things I hadn't felt since I was last with Ty.

"Have a seat."

Having gotten my bearings, I managed to sit down. Ty sat across from me, his blue eyes matching the waves that were at a lovely ebb and flow right next to us. Pushing aside the food so he could reach me, he took my hands in his.

"Are you surprised?" he asked.

I nodded. I was more than surprised. Touched. Loved. All were words that swarmed around in my mind. If I opened my mouth, I knew my tears would fall.

"Speechless?" He quirked his eyebrow and sat back in his chair. "I can't believe I made Lydia Duncan speechless."

I laughed as a tear fell down my face.

"Hey, none of that." Ty gently wiped the tear from my cheek.

"I'm just so stunned. You did all this for me? Why?" Normally I wasn't the type of woman who questioned when someone did something nice for her, but I couldn't help but wonder why, after all this time, Ty was acting like I'd never left. Like we hadn't broken each other's hearts.

Ty smiled. "There isn't much I wouldn't do for you. I wanted to show you that even after all these years, the way I feel about you hasn't changed. I'm not asking you to move here or any of that right now. I know you're grieving. Hell, I am too. But I am asking for right now. For this time we have together, to show you what we could be. Can you do that?"

There wasn't anything I wanted more than to let myself have these days with Ty and my family and to not think about what would happen when I left. I overanalyzed. I planned. I didn't do surprises. Not anymore. But right now, I would do just about anything to see Ty smile and look at me like he was. Like I was everything. *His* everything.

Cupping his face in my hands, I stared into the deep blue eyes of Ty Rue. "I can do that. I can't promise what will happen when I leave but right now, I'm yours."

I leaned in and brushed my lips against his. The softness that I remembered was perfection, the low growl in his throat vibrated our bodies. We didn't let up, we enjoyed the passion that we felt in each other's embrace, the kiss showing how much we still cared for each other.

When we parted, Ty stood up and opened the food.

I looked down at Chinese food and gawked. "How'd you get this?" There were no Chinese restaurants on the island.

"Your favorite place off island flies food over now." Ty had planned all of this for me and I fought with the lump of my throat. I wouldn't cry again, not all over my Orange Chicken.

We ate and had one of the best conversations I'd had in a while. We talked about my college days. And I had Ty clutching his chest in laughter telling him about the time I'd corrected the law professor and gotten kicked out of the classroom.

"You always had to argue." Ty shook his head.

"Hey! I wasn't arguing. It was the truth. He misreported facts. I couldn't have that." I smiled.

"What do you want to do now before we head in for our blood-and-gore marathon?" Ty rubbed his hands together. I looked out on the ocean and the glistening sand.

"Can we walk on the beach?"

"You read my mind."

Hand in hand, Ty and I walked on the beach, the waves brushing against our bare feet. It was cold, but I didn't mind because I had Ty to keep me warm, even if just for a while. My hair tangled around my face but I caught glimpses of Ty smiling as we walked the length of the beach. I was falling in love with Ty Rue all over again, and this time I wasn't sure I could let him go.

Chapter Fourteen

Ty

Lydia was mine. Even if just for the next week, but I counted that as a partial win. I wasn't sure where we would end up, but if I had my way we'd be married and expecting our first kid. Logistically, that wasn't possible, but I could dream.

"Do you want help cleaning up?" Lydia started stacking the plates and I stilled her hands.

"No. I've got this."

"If you're sure…" She hesitated.

"Justin and Geri are coming to clean it up," I said with a smile.

Lydia laughed. "You're a mess. Why would they do that?"

"Because people love you, Lyd. Geri wanted you to have this night just as much as I did. They came and helped set it all up with me too. People love you. Just because you left doesn't make that love turn off."

Lydia's chest heaved, her lips trembling.

"I'm going to take a shower." Lydia turned to walk away, and I couldn't shake the feeling that something was wrong.

"Hey!" Gently grabbing her arm, I pulled her against me. "What's wrong? Just a few minutes ago you were smiling. Now you're all glum."

"I have to go back to Boston Monday. Just for court, but I don't want to go. I don't want to leave any of this. Especially you." Her fingers traced my chin, stopping at my lips. Brushing a kiss against her lips, I smiled and tucked her hair behind her ear. The wind took it away again.

"It's okay. You'll be back after court, right?"

She nodded. "Yes, but..."

"There's nothing to worry about then. We'll be here." I pressed a kiss to her forehead. "We have always been here."

She sighed, relaxing into my embrace.

"Now go shower so I can corrupt your mind with *The Walking Dead*."

I watched her walk away into the cottage, taking little glances back every so often as though to make sure I was still here. I was here, I always would be, and it was about time she realized that.

* * * *

I was sitting on the couch, balancing a bowl of popcorn on my lap, when I heard the bathroom door creak open. Placing the bowl on the coffee table, I stood in the middle of the living room, clutching a chocolate rose in my hand.

After a few minutes, Lydia's footsteps carried down the hall and I tried to make myself look sexy. I puckered my lips and batted my eyelashes playfully, trying to lighten the mood. I didn't want everything to be so heavy with emotion. Granted, I wanted her to know how much she meant to me, but that didn't mean everything had to be a heart-to-heart with gushing words that took everything out of me. Tomorrow would bring enough emotion to last her a lifetime. I wanted tonight to be about her and making sure she was happy.

Lydia's hair was still wet and hung down her back. She was brushing it as she walked, and when she saw me she smiled, cautiously moving toward me.

"Is that a rose?" Taking it from my hand, she laughed. "A candy rose, real clever." She brought it to her nose and sniffed. "Smells delicious. Even better than the real thing."

"And it's more practical," I added. "Turn around. Let me help."

I took the brush from her hands, and Lydia turned her back to me. With gentle, slow movements, I brushed her hair.

"A girl could get used to this," she murmured.

"All right. I think that's good. Although, I'm no hair guru."

Lydia smoothed her hair with her hand. "Feels great. No tangles." She winked at me. Placing the brush on the coffee table, she sat in the middle of the couch, putting up her feet on the coffee table.

"This cottage is so freaking cute. I noticed something, though…" A hint of pink rushed across her cheeks.

"What's that?" I sat next to her and continued stroking her hair with my hand. It was so soft.

"There's one bedroom. Do you have some sort of alternate agenda here?" She eyeballed me, a bit of humor dancing in her eyes as she wiggled her finger.

"Why, little ol' me?" I gasped and brought my hand to my mouth. "I'm a gentleman and will be sleeping on the couch."

Lydia snuggled close to me, resting her head on my chest.

"Good, because I'm not sure I could handle sleeping next to you."

My hand stilled against her hair, and I wanted to ask her what she meant. Instead, I grabbed the remote and turned on the TV and clicked on Netflix. *Better to not open that door. Not yet.*

"Ready for the best show of your life?"

She laughed and took the popcorn off the table. "Let's do this. If I'm scarred for life, you're paying my therapy bills."

With a chuckle, I clicked play and let the marathon begin.

* * * *

"Oh my God, gross!" Lydia jumped and buried her head against my chest as a walker got slashed in the head. "Tell me when it's over," she said into my shirt, which she was clutching for dear life.

A few seconds later I gave her the all clear. "The episode's over and it's almost one in the morning. I think it's time for bed."

Lydia let go of my shirt and glanced up, her eyes still shut. "Is it really over?"

"Yes." I placed my lips on hers and felt her smile. "You're so cute when you're scared."

"I'm not scared." Lydia opened her eyes and stared into mine. "I just don't like to see brains splattered everywhere! It's perfectly natural to not want to see that. I think something's wrong with you!" She laughed.

We both stood up, both of us seemingly not wanting the evening to end.

"I had such a great time tonight, Ty. I'd forgotten t what it felt like."

"What?"

"Being with someone you care deeply about." She brushed a kiss to my cheek. "Good night. Thank you for tonight. I'll never forget it."

Snatching the chocolate rose off the table, she grinned at me. "In case I need a late-night snack."

Lydia walked away, bringing the rose to her nose again and taking a sniff. I heard the bedroom door shut with a click.

"I love you," I whispered into the air, hoping that the ocean breeze that was coming from the open windows would carry the message.

Fluffing the pillows on the too-hard couch, and cursing myself for not remembering to grab the spare blankets from the bedroom closet, I lay down and stared at the ceiling.

Sleep didn't come easily. My thoughts were overrun with the kisses Lydia and I had shared and her promise to be mine for the time she was here. As my eyes shut the last thing I saw was her beautiful face.

* * * *

"Ty. Are you awake?" I bolted up, almost knocking Lydia over in the process. She stood next to the couch, huddled in an oversized sweater and leggings. Her face was scrunched into a scowl as she looked frantically all around her.

"What's wrong?"

Her lower lip quivered. "I'm scared," she whined.

Throwing my head back, I laughed.

"Stop!" She stomped her foot. "It's not funny. I keep thinking zombies are going to jump out of the closet or something. It's all your fault!"

"I'm sorry. Didn't know you were still a scaredy cat."

She sucked in a sharp breath. "I am not a scaredy cat."

"I remember watching *IT* with you and Dylan, when you spilled popcorn all over us."

She rolled her eyes. "I was ten. You guys were evil and told me it was a happy movie about clowns."

"Fair enough. But some things never change." I tugged her hair.

"Sleep with me?" She leaned into my touch, causing my fingertips to brush the bare skin of her neck.

"Ah…"

"Get your head out of the gutter." She swatted my arm. "Next to me in the bed. I'll feel safe. I always feel safe when you're around."

My heart thumped loudly and I glanced down, prepared to see it jump out of my chest. She felt safe with me.

"When you put it that way…" As I slung her over my shoulder, she squealed. I carried her to the bedroom.

"Put me down! You're crazy!" She playfully hit my back.

Tossing her onto the bed, I crawled in next to her and snuggled into the blankets.

"Come on. Don't get shy on me now." I patted the empty side of the bed.

"I like that side of the bed." She pointed to where I was lying.

"You, Lydia Duncan, are a pain in my butt." I scooted over.

"Thank you." She cuddled in next to me, resting her head in the crock of my arm. "Is this okay?"

"This is perfect." Our eyes met and Lydia offered me a sleepy smile. I turned off the bedside light and relished the darkness.

The outline of Lydia's face was still visible even in the dark, and I listened to her breathing change, her soft snores soon filling the room. The smile never left her face and when she snuggled in closer, clutching my shirt as she drifted deeper into sleep, I said it again.

"I love you, Lydia."

"I love you, too," she muttered.

I looked down at her. She was asleep, and I wasn't sure whether she even knew what she'd said. But I held onto those words, and replayed them repeatedly as I drifted into my own peaceful sleep with the woman I loved in my arms. And whether it had been her subconscious speaking for her or not, deep down, she loved me too.

Chapter Fifteen

Lydia

Nothing prepares you for the day you have to say goodbye to a parent. My father raised me and guided me into the person that I was. Without him, I know I would have never pursued my dream to go to law school. He'd bought me my very first law book at only nine years old. My mother had told him he was being ridiculous and that nine-year-old girls wanted dolls, not law books. She couldn't have been more wrong.

"William, she's a nine-year-old girl. Buy her a Barbie or something, not a law book."

My father ignored her and patted the seat next to him on the couch. "Come sit."

I ran to the couch and held out my hands greedily. He placed the book in my hands and I stroked the cover — Constitutional Law for Kids.

"Don't let anyone tell you that you can't do something, okay?"

I nodded. "Open it up! Read me some." I snuggled into my dad's arms and he opened the first page and started reading.

That had become our routine every Sunday, until I'd left for college. He'd listen to me read various law books, and while he'd usually fallen asleep, it had been my most favorite time of week.

I held *Constitutional Law for Kids* in my hands as I sat on the edge of the bed.

"No wonder your bag was so heavy," Ty said as the bed dipped next to me.

"It's the first law book I ever got. My dad gave it to me."

Ty's phone buzzed. He looked at the incoming message and gripped my knee. "It's time to get ready."

"I wish we could stay here longer." I held the book close to my chest. The memory flitted in and out of my mind, but my focus shifted to how close Ty was to me. I could feel the heat radiating off him. Sleeping in his arms was something I'd never gotten the chance to do when we were younger. We had just been kids, after all. We had talked about buying a cottage like this one together and falling asleep in each other's arms to the sound of waves. Ty had made our childhood dream a reality. He'd made all my dreams a reality, even by letting go. Although it hurt to have lived the past decade without him, by letting me get on that boat he'd let me pursue my dream, he'd given me up. So I could live.

"I got the cottage for the weekend. I figured some of your family would stay longer and you could use an escape."

I breathed out a sigh of relief. I had a place to escape to when everything became too much. I was already getting overwhelmed, and the memorial service hadn't even started yet.

Ty kissed my forehead, wrapped me in a hug and left the bedroom so I could get dressed.

I went through the motions, curling my hair so I looked presentable, applying makeup, including water-proof mascara. I was ready to lay my father to rest.

I stepped out of the bedroom and wandered the cottage looking for Ty. I found him standing outside on the small porch, his hands shoved in his pants pockets.

His back was to me, the white dress shirt he was wearing taut across his back. Wrapping my arms around him, I pressed myself against him.

"Hey." He placed his hands over mine where they rested against his chest. "You okay?"

"I am now." Ty's cologne mixed with the subtle hint of candy that seemed to follow him everywhere greeted me. "You smell like soap and chocolate."

Ty laughed. "I wouldn't be a good candy store owner unless I did."

I knew it was time. Hand in hand we walked toward his truck and headed to say goodbye to William Duncan. My father.

* * * *

"If anyone would like to say anything before we send William off to rest, please step forward."

My mother stood hunched next to Dylan. He swayed side to side, in sync with the wind, which was relentless. It was as if it knew what was happening. It waited for my father, to take him away to where he would be at peace.

A few people came forward and spoke about how funny he had been. How kind. They were all great words. Words that would have made my father huff and tell people to stop fussing over him. But they were true because he had been funny and kind. Everyone on the island had looked up to him and known that if they ever needed anything, my father would be there.

"I'd like to say something." My hands shook and Dylan gripped my waist as if to steady me. As he brushed a kiss to my temple, everyone stared at us. My mom offered me a sad smile as I took my father's ashes from her hands.

"William Duncan, my father." My voice cracked and I cleared my throat. "He was everything that all of you said. He was funny, kind and outgoing. An outstanding cop and an overall good person. But he was more than that." I rubbed my hands over the urn. "William was a dreamer, just like me. He dreamed of better things for me, a life outside of this island. He wanted me to be happy and knew that staying here wouldn't allow me to pursue all my potential, so he let me go." Tears streamed down my face and they dried as the wind crashed around us. The tide was coming in and I knew any minute it would be at our feet. "He let me go knowing that someday I'd be back because this island, even though I felt stifled by its smallness, by the fact that everyone knew everyone else's business, this island was home. His most favorite place in the entire world. Now it's time to make my father a permanent part of the place he loved the most."

Walking away from the crowd, I heard Dylan tell my mother to stay behind as I headed toward the water. It was freezing, the fall chill causing it to turn cold. The subtle warmness that the summer brought to the water was gone but I could swear I felt it the deeper I got. My father had taught me to swim on this beach. He and my mother had gotten married on this beach. Everything was coming full circle. My father would be laid to rest on this beach.

I opened the urn, the wind slowing down and the water settling around me.

"I love you, Dad. Thank you for being the best dad a girl could ask for." With a flick of my wrist, I watched my father's ashes dance in the wind. Splashes of water caught my attention and I looked over my shoulder to where Ty stood next to me.

"You're going to get pneumonia," he said as he put his arms around me.

"So are you." I smiled in between my tears.

"You know he'll always be with you. In the breeze. In the sand. In the salt air that greets you every morning when you step outside. Your father is everywhere and he's so proud of you." The wind picked up, as if my father were trying to tell me that he agreed.

"Come on. I don't want you to catch a man cold." I smirked.

Ty splashed me and I jumped on him, forcing him under the water. Shivering, we ran toward the beach to get warm, our laughter following us.

The day had been filled with sadness and heartache. Having to say goodbye was never easy. But underneath it all, there was hope. A subtle wish that this could be my normal. Surrounded by the people that meant so much to me. A calmness settled deep within me as Ty and I sloshed out of the water, my mother fussing over us. No matter where I went, what position I held or how hard I tried to make myself a city girl, this island, these people, would forever be my home.

Chapter Sixteen

Ty

Today was more of a celebration than a memorial. After William's ashes were scattered in the ocean, everyone headed to the restaurant to eat, drink and remember William as he would have wanted to be remembered. Not with tears and sadness, but with laughter, beer and good food.

I had piled my plate with surf and turf, eating more than my fair share. It had been William's favorite. Just like the chocolate mousse pie that I'd eaten, and the lemon meringue pie. I was officially stuffed.

"Crazy how many people showed up, huh?" Dylan slid next to me and handed me a drink. "Your hands are empty. My dad wouldn't want that." He smiled as he took a swig of his beer.

"It's nuts. What, there have to be a hundred people here at least." I tried to count but my eyes went fuzzy at the people grouped together near the bar, and still others were milling around outside on the beach enjoying the beautiful fall night.

"Can't say my dad wasn't loved. It's going to be weird without him." Dylan spun his beer around in his hands.

Geri stood across the restaurant, eyeballing Dylan and me as she chatted with Justin. He played with the ends of her rainbow hair. Leaning in, he whispered something that made her smile. But her eyes never left Justin.

"That was nice of you to invite Geri." I smirked as I brought the beer to my mouth.

"For Lydia," Dylan added with a cough. He fidgeted with his shirt, yanking it down before quickly looking at Geri, who tried to pretend that she hadn't been staring at him.

"Right, for Lydia. The way she's been looking at you all night, I'm sure it was just for Lydia."

Dylan gave me the middle finger and promptly polished off his beer.

"Don't ask because I'm not telling. I promised I wouldn't say a thing," Dylan said as he pushed off the wall. "I should mingle but my God do I want to just get drunk on the beach and stare at the stars. Remember those days? Minus the beer, of course."

"Who says we can't do that now?" I caught sight of Lydia out of the corner of my eye and waved her over. Despite the mood of the party, the atmosphere surrounding Dylan, Lydia, Geri and me was off. We needed something to jar things up. Something that would bring us all together, even if just for a bit. I knew we had all grown up and gone our separate ways, but friendships like what we'd shared were always there. Maybe a bit tempered, but I knew deep down our friendship would never die. No matter where our lives took us.

"Hey." Lydia snaked her arms around my waist and Dylan made a dramatic gagging sound.

"Does this mean you two are together? Again?" He said "again" dramatically, like we had broken up a zillion times. It was just once, and in my book that had been one time too many.

"Just seeing where things take us while I'm home." Lydia stood on her tiptoes and placed a kiss to my lips. I wanted things to be forever. For her to realize that I was and always would be hers. As much as I didn't want to get my hopes up, her words, they gave me hope. They made me fall in love with her even more.

"I still can't believe my best friend fell in love with my sister." Dylan glanced at Lydia, who was staring up at me. I caught a hint of sadness in his eyes when he looked at her but it was quickly replaced with a smile. "And my little sister fell in love with my best friend."

Lydia smiled but didn't correct him.

"So, what do you guys want?" Lydia asked as she placed her hands on her slender hips. "You two look like you're up to something." She pointed between us.

"Us? Ty and I never get into trouble." Dylan smirked. It was amazing that he'd become a cop like William, because Dylan had always been the mastermind behind all the crazy stuff we'd done as kids. But just like he'd known how to get us into trouble, he'd known how to get us out of it. *Most of the time.*

We saw the lights of the cop car as we cowered behind the funeral home. Geri had gone with us this time, and she'd found an open window. She'd gone inside and set off the alarm.

"Come out, kids. I know you're there." Mr. Duncan's voice carried over the trees and Lydia looked at me. She wasn't scared of her father, but she always feared disappointing him.

Dylan walked out, then me and Geri. Lydia clung to the tree for dear life.

"You too, Lyd." Mr. Duncan didn't seem mad. I thought I even caught a smile pass across his face.

"I think she's afraid." Dylan snickered.

"Hush it. You're all in big trouble," Mr. Duncan said.

Geri hung her head, clearly taking most of the blame on herself because she'd been the one who'd ventured inside.

"In our defense, we noticed the opened window and tried to lift Geri to close it and she fell in." Lydia came out, her head held high. Oh, she was good.

"Lydia, I wasn't born yesterday. What would all four of you be out here looking for at ten o'clock at night?" Mr. Duncan shook his head.

"Stargazing," Lydia said without missing a beat. Dylan and Geri smirked.

Mr. Duncan sighed, and we all watched as he clearly struggled with what to do.

"Get out of here. Go stargaze or whatever you claim you were doing. If I catch you guys snooping around here again…"

"You won't," Lydia said. Mr. Duncan got into his squad car and drove away.

"Catch us that is!" Dylan said as he rubbed his hands together. "What can we get into now?"

We'd lived our youth pushing the limits. We never did anything extremely illegal, nothing that would land us behind bars. But I'd loved our times together.

Stargazing or sneaking into funeral homes, they had been some of the best times of my life.

"How about we grab as many beers as we can carry, snag the blankets out of the back of my truck and head out to the beach and watch the stars?" I quirked my eyebrow.

"I'd say heck yes! I'll grab Geri and Justin."

I noticed Dylan's face drop at the sound of Justin's name. I didn't push him anymore about him and Geri but there was something there, anyone could see it.

Lydia and Geri worked on getting beers and Dylan and I gathered the blankets from the back of my truck. Living on the island, I had a trunk full of odds and ends. You never knew when you'd go to the beach, need blankets, a cooler, water or chairs. I was stocked and prepared at all times.

We set up high enough on the beach where the tide wouldn't reach us, but close enough where you could still hear the waves. Dylan and I laid out a few blankets. One for Lydia and me, and two others. I suspected Dylan was prepared for Geri and Justin to saddle up together.

"Hey!" Lydia bounced down the beach, Geri right on her heels. "We're here!" She flopped down next to me and emptied out the contents of her bag. There were beers and snacks. Various chips and candies. I kissed her temple as she organized everything into piles.

"Where's Justin?" Dylan asked, stretching out his legs, clearly trying to seem only half interested.

"He had to work," Geri said as she sat down next to him.

I noticed he stiffened at the closeness of her. Geri rested her hand on his knee and his shoulders relaxed. Scooting over, he swiped a beer. Dylan was serious about the getting drunk part. I'd counted he'd had at least three beers at the restaurant already.

"Bummer," Dylan said with a small smile as he brought the beer to his lips.

Yeah, he liked her. Darn shame he wouldn't do something about it.

"It's just like old times." Lydia lay down and placed her head in my lap. She stared up at the sky just as the sun was starting to set. It was stunning, the various oranges and reds that stretched across the sky.

"Except I'm not pining for you." Lydia's soft laugh shook my legs.

"No need. You already have me," I replied. She snuggled in closer.

"Do you guys remember when I got stung by a jellyfish?" Geri shuddered. "I swear I was going to die."

Lydia sat up and exhaled loudly. "Oh yeah. I almost forgot about that." She giggled.

"Not me. Scarred me for life." Geri lifted up her skirt and showed a scar on her thigh. "Literally."

"How'd you manage to stop the stinging anyway? I can't remember. Lydia and I ran to get help and when we came back you weren't screaming bloody murder anymore?" I asked.

Geri blushed.

Dylan coughed. "I peed on it."

"What?" Lydia gasped. "You *peed* on Geri?" She looked to me for an explanation but I just shrugged before going into a fit of laughter. I laughed so hard tears streamed down my face.

"Wow. That just makes the story even better. Never knew that happened." I wiped the tears away.

"I don't typically go around telling people I was peed on. It wasn't one of my finest moments." Geri repositioned herself so she was lying on her stomach, her feet dangling behind her. "But this? Laying under the stars with my best friends from high school? I never forgot this."

Lydia lay down next to her, wrapping her arm around her shoulders. I raised my beer to Dylan — we didn't usually cuddle — as a token of my affection for him. No bromance. Just a solid love for the kid who had been with me forever and grown up like a brother to me.

"What happened to the moon? It wasn't supposed to be cloudy tonight." Lydia glanced up and gasped. I looked up, and a guy stood in front of us. He gave a small wave before shoving his hands into his pockets.

"Lee?" Lydia's mouth hung open.

I thought they weren't dating? Why would he show up here unannounced?

"Hey, Lydia," he said.

I hated that he was wearing a suit on the beach, his shiny black dress shoes covered in sand. I hated that his hair was slicked back, not a piece out of place. More so, I hated that he was here. Lydia stood up quickly, brushing off sand.

"What are you doing here?"

She looked at him, confusion dripping from her face as her brows scrunched together. I could tell she was trying to make sense out of what was happening. Dylan and Geri looked at me and I shrugged. I knew who he was. But just like Lydia, I had no idea what he was doing here. I so badly wanted to be a jerk and ignore Lee, stay lying on my blanket, looking at the stars and getting drunk. Instead, I stood up, shook his hand and introduced myself, secretly hoping that he wasn't here to take Lydia away.

Chapter Seventeen

Lydia

What the hell? I had absolutely no idea why Lee was here. I hadn't asked him to come or given any hints that I needed him here so why he'd thought coming was a good idea was beyond me. By the looks that Ty and my brother were giving him, they didn't know why he was here either. I wasn't ungrateful that he'd come, just confused. I also knew Dylan and Ty would give him a hard time.

"I came because it was your father's memorial today. Looks like I missed it. You know, work and all." Lee frowned and looked at Ty's hand, which was reached out for mine. I was halfway between angry and touched. Who didn't want a man to travel and be there for them when their father passed? But it was all wrong, merging my two worlds together. Lee looked incredibly uncomfortable in his suit and his dress shoes that were sinking into the sand. His hair was so plastered down it didn't even blow in the breeze. He just looked flat-out uncomfortable.

"Give me a minute, guys," I told Dylan, Geri and Ty. Grabbing Lee by the arm, I led him away from the crowd and down the beach.

"Why do I get the feeling that I made a mistake coming here? I thought that I was being a good friend. I know we don't talk a lot about our personal lives but I know you loved your family." Lee let out an odd laugh and kicked the sand. "Didn't want you to be alone."

"I appreciate you coming. I do. But I'm not alone."

"Clearly." Lee grunted as he looked back at Ty and Dylan, who were staring at us.

I sighed and placed my hand on Lee's chest. I was going about this all wrong. I didn't want to push Lee away when he was being so kind but I also didn't want to give mixed signals.

"I'm sorry. I don't mean to be ungrateful. Have you eaten? You must be exhausted." I gave him a smile. A truce. All I could offer to show my appreciation for him being here.

"No. I came right over on the boat after work. It's been crazy lately."

"Well, let's get you something to eat and we can worry about the rest later."

Lee leaned in and tucked a stray piece of hair behind my ear. His fingers gently brushed my cheek. They felt foreign. Cold. They weren't Ty's. Nothing about Lee came remotely close to Ty. I found him attractive, but what I wanted was the boy who had asked me out under the stars. The boy who had kissed me for the first time and told me he loved me as my toes froze in the snow. I didn't want pressed suits and fancy shoes. I wanted simple. Jeans and a T-shirt.

I wanted Ty.

I looked back at where Dylan, Ty and Geri had been and saw that they were walking back toward the restaurant. Lee and I trekked up the sand to meet them with the hopes of snagging him some food.

"So, who are they? You all seem close," Lee said as he piled food on his plate. I couldn't keep him away from them forever. I felt their eyes boring into me.

"Come on. I'll introduce you." I walked in front of Lee, him trailing behind, balancing his food as we maneuvered through the people.

Dylan, Ty and Geri stood at the bar, smiles stretched across their faces. *This was going to be fun.*

"Hey, guys. Sorry for sneaking away. Everyone, this is Lee. Lee, that guy there is my older brother, Dylan. The rainbow princess is my best friend Geri and this guy," I tugged on Ty's shirt, "is Ty Rue. But You already knew that since he was the only one to introduce himself." I glared at Dylan and Geri, who shrugged and tipped back their beers.

"Nice to meet you all," Lee said with a wave.

"How do you know my sister?" Dylan flexed his muscles as he crossed his arms across his chest.

"Dylan, don't," I warned. He always had to be a jerk to every guy who ever tried to date me. Except Ty. He'd said Ty already knew that he could kick his butt.

"We went to law school together. Been friends ever since."

Lee glanced up briefly from his phone, which he'd been attached to since we'd gotten to the bar. I don't know how he managed to hold his plate full of food and text at the same time, but he'd mastered it.

I had been like that, glued to my phone, not wanting to miss a message or email. Heaven forbid someone had to wait for a reply.

Geri shook her head and made an ugly face, clearly not approving of Lee.

"And you came here why?" Dylan asked. Ty choked on his beer. These two were something else.

"I came because I knew her father passed and the memorial service was today. I didn't want her to be alone." Lee looked at me and winked. Geri pretended she was throwing up. Thank goodness Lee was too enthralled with his phone to notice everyone acting like children.

"You missed the memorial. It was at four." Ty finally spoke, his eyes never leaving mine.

"I know. Feel terrible, but I had to work a last-minute case. You know, being a lawyer can make it really hard to plan things." Lee laughed like what he'd said would win him some comedy award. I laughed a bit so it wouldn't be so awkward.

"I wouldn't know. I own a candy store," Ty said.

Lee cocked his head to the side and studied Ty for a minute. He sized him up, clearly not caring if he noticed.

"That sounds fun." He snickered.

Dylan clenched his fists at his sides and Ty just smiled, leaning against the bar.

"It is fun, because I can spend time with my friends and family without being glued to a cell phone. I have priorities beyond just work. It makes my life much more fulfilling."

Lee's face turned beet red and he opened his mouth to protest but Geri cut him off.

"Where are you staying, Lee?"

Geri grinned at me as she asked. I bit my bottom lip. I hadn't thought of that.

"I never thought that far ahead. Is there a Hilton or something around here? I'd like to earn some points if I can." He looked around like one would manifest from thin air.

"Ah, no. This is Nantucket, not New York or Boston or wherever the heck you're from. The inn is probably booked because of the memorial. Looks like you get to shack up with me." Dylan slapped Lee on the shoulders. He tensed and almost dropped his plate.

"Where are you staying, Lydia?" Lee looked at me expectantly.

"With me," Ty said.

And silence.

Ty and Lee had some manly stare-off and I swear one of them was about to sling me over their shoulder and swing away with me like I was Jane and they were Tarzan.

I clapped my hands together, the tension in the air becoming too much. "Why don't we head to the cottage for a bit and we can hang out. It's all dying down here anyways." I glanced around at the few stragglers who were drinking a bit too much or going for thirds at the buffet.

"I'm game," Ty said as he shot himself off the bar.

"Me too. Ohh! I can dye my hair!"

Lee looked at Geri with disgust and I wanted to punch him in the face. I'd never seen this side of him. The pretentious, 'hold your nose up at anything that isn't pressed and perfect' side.

"You know what? I've been meaning to dye my hair too." As I wrapped my arm through Geri's, Lee texted and walked—which should be outlawed because he ran into two people and tripped over a chair—and Dylan and Ty held up the rear, their heads close together as they spoke in soft tones. They were up to something, and I knew that whatever it was would solidify the fact that Lee would never want to speak to me again.

* * * *

We all piled into the cottage, where the remnants of the night before were still scattered about.

"Someone had a good time last night." Geri winked at me.

Ty and Dylan stayed out on the porch, I'm sure plotting whatever they were going to do to Lee. The poor guy didn't know what was coming. I could have warned him, but he'd decided to come to Nantucket, and now he was going to get the full welcome.

Lee plopped down on the couch and took off his suit jacket. He was handsome, there was no denying that, but now that I saw him in my world, a world that wasn't a courtroom or fancy upscale restaurant, he didn't fit.

"What happened last night?" Lee asked with a smile, like he was interested.

"Ty totally won this one over with a romantic dinner on the beach and a *Walking Dead* marathon." Geri said.

Lee glared at me. I shrugged and popped a chocolate-covered peanut in my mouth. There was no guilt. I wasn't beholden to Lee and had made it perfectly clear that I wasn't looking for a relationship.

"You really think you want to dye your hair?" Geri asked, trying to change the subject.

"Mmhm. I can't have any of those funky colors though."

"Yeah. Plus, I like a woman with plain hair," Lee added.

Geri stuck out her tongue at him but he missed it due to his face being buried in his phone.

"Come on. I'm dying your hair." Geri tugged on my arm and we went into the bathroom.

"I'm not sure about this…" I hesitated as she sat me down on the toilet and started pulling out stuff from her bag.

"Don't worry. I'll make it subtle. You won't look like a My Little Pony like me."

I watched her mix the color and felt my throat go dry. I'd never done anything like this before. I'd never even dyed my hair. But part of me wanted this. It was a small thing, but it signified so much for me. Change. Spontaneity. And I wanted it all. I was tired of the pressed suits and high heels that gave me blisters. My vision that blurred after only being awake for a few hours because I was glued to my phone or laptop. I wanted something different for a change, even if just to add some color to my hair.

"All right. Let's do this!" Geri smiled and stepped back and looked at me like she was painting one of her pictures.

"Close your eyes. I'm going to make you fabulous."

* * * *

Walking into the living room like she was on a catwalk, Geri bowed then cleared her throat.

"I would like to present the new and improved Lydia Duncan!" I heard a few claps as I walked out and did a spin. The tips of my hair were dyed a deep pink and I loved it. I felt different. Alive in an odd, rebellious way. This was a solid screw you to the strict routine that I had to keep. I was a rebel. Sort of. Well, as much as my pink hair made me.

"You look beautiful." Ty stood up and cupped my cheeks with his hands. Looking into his eyes was like looking into the sun—it was so bright it was blinding, but once you got used to it, there was nowhere else you'd rather look. I wanted the warmth that radiated from his eyes.

"Thank you." I smiled.

"Franklin is going to have a field day with that." Lee chuckled.

"Let him have a field day. It's tasteful and she looks gorgeous," Geri said with her hands on her hips. Lee put up his hands in defeat and slung his feet on the coffee table, showcasing his argyle socks. They were color-coordinated with his suit. Could he be any more perfect?

I caught Lee looking at me out of the corner of his eye, watching Ty's hands play with my newly colored hair.

"I need to crash. I'm in no shape to be driving." Dylan stood up and swayed side to side.

"None of us should be driving," Ty said. "Everyone can crash here. I think there's an air mattress in the closet. The girls can take the bed." Ty smirked. I narrowed my eyes at him.

"Be nice." I pressed my finger to his chest.

"I'm always nice." He grinned. "Now Dylan on the other hand…" I looked over at my brother, who was staring at Lee with a sinister smile on his face.

"No funny business." I shook her finger at him.

Geri put her arm around my shoulders. "Where's the fun in that? It's a rite of passage. You sleep over with our crew, the first to fall asleep gets pranked." She shrugged like it was a rule that couldn't be broken.

"Just don't shave anything on his face." I sighed. Although, I did fight back a smile at the thought of Lee without any eyebrows.

"Okay, no shaving eyebrows. We can manage that." Dylan was dragging the air mattress out of the closet and Lee had managed to put his phone down long enough to move the coffee table out of the way.

"Promise?"

"Promise." Ty smirked. "Need me to tuck you in?"

"Ugh, gross. She's mine tonight. You can have her for the rest of your life." Geri pulled me toward the bedroom. I shimmied out of her grasp and ran back to Ty and kissed him. I moaned against his mouth, everything that I had been missing for the past ten years coming through the kiss. I was weightless, free of all my deadlines and the regimented routine that I kept. I was flying and Ty was right next to me.

Ty and I stood in the hallway, our chests heaving, our lips swollen from the kiss that we'd just shared.

Pressing his forehead against mine, he smiled. "There she is."

"Who?" I asked.

"The girl I fell in love with."

"You love me?" I played with the hem of his shirt. I needed to focus on anything other than the way my heart was beating. Slow. Like the dance that Ty and I had shared in the bar. Just us. No one else.

"Never stopped, Lyd."

"What if I told you that I love you too? That even when I fought against how much I missed home and missed you, that it was fruitless."

"I'd say okay." He stilled my hands, which were still playing with the hem of his shirt.

"I love you," I said before I lost my nerve.

"Okay." Ty smiled and brought my hands to his lips. "Go to bed, sweetheart. I'll be here when you wake up and you can tell me you love me again." He kissed my lips. "And again." He kissed me once more. "And again."

Backing away, my body aching to be close to Ty's again, I wanted to get to sleep so I could wake up and hear him tell me he loved me. Because no matter how many times he said it, I never tired of hearing it. Those words were what I had been missing.

Chapter Eighteen

Ty

Lee was sprawled out, his arm hanging off the couch. His face was scrunched into a scowl. Even in his sleep I wanted to flick him on his ear and tell him to lighten the heck up. The poor guy was wound so tight. His cell phone was balanced on his chest and his other hand grasped it for dear life.

"I don't like him," Dylan said as he sprayed shaving cream in Lee's free hand.

"You don't know him." I slowly pried Lee's phone out of his hand. "What do you say we hide this and watch him squirm looking for it?"

Dylan's face lit up. "For someone who says I don't know him, you don't seem too fond of him either."

"He likes your sister. I'm sure he came here as some gallant act to woo her." I grunted.

Dylan clutched his chest. "I just pictured him riding in on a horse."

"You're drunk." Smiling, I shook my head.

"Yeeep. Still, he's all wrong for Lydia. Look at his suit. He wore dress shoes to the beach. At least take them off. Put your toes in the sand! It's the best part," he screeched. Lee stirred and we both stood still, fearful that he would wake up. When he sighed and his eyes stayed closed, we both were able to relax.

"Trust me, I know he's all wrong for her," I said.

"Then why are you just letting him drool over her? He's like a dog in heat." Dylan poked Lee's face.

"Because Lydia loves me, not him. She's made that clear." I wrapped Lee's phone in a towel and stuffed it up in the fireplace. *Let him try to find it now.*

"Well, I hope Mr. Suit and Tie here realizes that before I have to put him in jail." Dylan put shaving cream on Lee's other hand, now that it was free from his phone.

"You can't put him in jail for liking your sister." I laughed.

"Try me! I'm the law!" Dylan started dancing and I knew he was two seconds away from passing out. Shaving cream dribbled on the floor.

"I haven't seen you drink this much since high school prom. You good?" I led him to the air mattress and laid him down.

"I'm about as good as a man who just buried his father and is watching the girl of his dreams fall for someone else could be," Dylan mumbled before promptly snoring.

"Wow," I said.

There it was. Lee was in love with Geri.

Crawling onto my corner of the air mattress, I fell asleep easily. I wasn't worried about Lee being here or Lydia having feelings for him. She loved me, and that was enough for me to trust that what we had would overcome anything that got thrown our way.

* * * *

I felt a kick to the air mattress and opened my eyes to see Geri standing over Dylan and me with her arms crossed.

"What?" I asked with a yawn.

"Lee's in there yelling at Lydia because of your prank." Dylan and I looked at each other and sat up. I rubbed my face, hoping that the tiredness I felt would go away.

"He's mad? It wasn't anything bad. Just some shaving cream," Dylan said.

"Yep. I'm disappointed in you guys. I expected something more epic. Shave his head or something. I'd loved to have seen his face when he looked in the mirror and saw his precious blond locks shaved." Geri grinned. She could be really scary sometimes.

"He hasn't noticed his phone missing yet, has he?" I smirked.

"Oh. Got him where it really hurts. I knew I liked you." Geri stared at Dylan, and I realized she was checking him out. He must have taken his shirt off during the night because he was shirtless, and Geri couldn't take his eyes off him.

"I'm going to save Lydia. I'll be back." Geri took my spot on the air mattress and I hoped that whatever was going on between them, or not, would work itself out. I'd never seen Dylan so hung up on a woman before.

"Morning." I knocked on the half-closed door to the bedroom before entering. I saw Lydia sitting on the bed with Lee pacing back and forth.

"Shaving cream? Really?" Lydia looked at me, clearly trying to be stern, but the tips of her lips fought with the desire to turn into a smile.

"Harmless prank." Lee stopped pacing and stood between Lydia and me. His dress shirt was untucked and wrinkled from sleep. "Harmless. More like childish," Lee said between his teeth.

"Hey now, Lee, it was all in good fun. That's what we do." Lydia pulled her hair on top of her head and placed it in a ponytail.

"That's not what *we* do. I'm a lawyer. Thirty years old. Not a teenager."

"I think you're blowing this out of proportion. I'm sorry if we offended you, it's just what we do here." I went to grab his shoulder to offer some sort of apology.

He stepped back. "And you two." Lee pointed between us. "This is why you never said yes to dating me."

Lydia stood up and moved toward me. I held my breath because while she had told me she loved me last night, maybe she wasn't ready to say it out loud to Lee. Or to anyone. Those words were still mine, though, regardless of what happened.

"It's always been Ty for me. We fell in love long ago."

I looked down at Lydia and my heart soared. We had fallen in love long ago and had never stopped. The type of love that we shared wasn't something that just went away. A decade or not.

"Wow. I wish you would have told me. I feel like a real tool coming here and trying to win you over when your heart clearly was never mine to win." Lee let out a laugh.

"I tried to forget. It was easier than remembering the times where there were no deadlines and projects. Courtrooms and suits. Here on the island, it's so different. "

"I can see that," Lee said as he looked at our entwined bodies.

"Hey, man, no hard feelings. You're a good friend for coming out here to make sure Lydia was okay. You're here now so let us show you around the island. It's a cool place. It'll grow on you. You won't want to leave."

Lee frowned. "Well, I am here. Do you mind if I stay?" He looked at Lydia.

"Of course not. You've always been a good friend and I hope we can stay that way."

Lee got lost in thought for a moment, clearly weighing what she just said.

"I'd like that. I'm sorry about being such a jerk. I got a huge contract for the new manufacturing corporation that opened up in Boston. It's going to be lots of travel, as they have offices all over the world, but I'm excited."

"That's so great, Lee. I'm proud of you." She gave him a quick hug.

"On that note, where can a guy get a cup of coffee around here?" Lee raised his eyebrow.

"We have a Starbucks!" Lydia said excitedly.

"Thank God!" Lee laughed. He stopped and everything went quiet. The faint sound of a phone ringing could be heard out in the living room. "Do you hear that? It's my phone." Lee bolted out of the room. "Has anyone seen my phone?" Lee's voice carried into the bedroom.

"What did you do with his phone?" Lydia asked with a smirk.

"What? Why do you think it's me?" I tried to hide my smile.

"I know you." She traced shapes on my chest with her finger. "You're a troublemaker and steal girls' hearts."

"Only heart I ever wanted to steal was yours, baby." I tackled her back onto the bed. Lydia went into a fit of giggles as I sprinkled kisses all over her face.

"I love you, Ty."

I smiled so wide I thought my face would break.

"What?" she asked.

"I couldn't wait to wake up to hear you say that again."

"I'll say it forever," Lydia said.

Banging at the door made Lydia jump.

"All right there, love birds. I'm not ready to be an uncle yet, so wrap it up and come help us find Lee's phone before he starts crying," Dylan said.

Lydia giggled and blushed, burying her face in my chest.

"I don't want to get up. You're so warm." Lydia sighed.

"Like you said, we have forever. Let's go help Lee find his phone."

Lydia stood up and put her hands on her hips. "You know where it is!"

Grinning, I brushed a kiss to her cheek. "Where's the fun in giving away my hiding spot?"

Shaking her head, Lydia headed out into the living room. The sound of Lee's frantic voice caused my chest to rumble with laughter. This poor guy was one step away from a retirement home.

There was nothing like a few days on the island to loosen someone up, and that's exactly what we all needed. Time together to remember when all we'd had to think about was the next fun thing we could do and how not to get caught. Everyone deserved that kind of experience at least once in their life. It helped put things into perspective that while making a name for yourself, whether it be as an artist or a partner in a law firm, friends and family, they believed in you from the beginning, even when you didn't believe in yourself. Years could separate the next time that we were all together again, but we had today. And today was all that mattered.

Chapter Nineteen

Lydia

There was so much that I wanted to do. I wanted to walk Main Street and hit up all the stores again. Visit the ice cream shop and get a heaping of ice cream, slathered in sprinkles. But most of all I wanted to do it with Geri, Dylan, Ty, even Lee by my side.

I wasn't expecting Lee to show up, that much was true, but now that he was here, I thought Ty had a great idea of showing him around and maybe helping him loosen up a bit. Maybe we could get him to remove the stick that had been up his butt.

"We should start a fire before we head out," Geri suggested as she started piling in the firewood.

"No!" Dylan and Ty said simultaneously.

I narrowed my eyes at them and pulled out my cell phone.

"Lee, do me a favor and stand by that fireplace," I instructed. He was currently one step away from ripping all the cabinets off the walls to find his phone.

I dialed his number and Lee bent down and shoved his hand inside of the fireplace. With a few pats and grunts, and some ash falling on his face, he pulled out his cell phone.

"Well would you look at that. I had no idea that was in there," Dylan said, obviously trying to hide the smile on his face.

"You're a darn police officer and sometimes I wonder how you even managed that." I playfully smacked him with my hand.

"Because I'm good at eating donuts?" Dylan rubbed his stomach, which didn't have an ounce of fat on it.

"I'm so sorry, Lee." I watched him wipe the ash from his face with the bottom of his shirt.

"It's okay." He smiled. For the first time since he'd gotten here, it didn't feel awkward.

"So, what are we doing today?" Geri clapped her hands together. "I want to get some sun."

"It's like sixty degrees outside," Ty said as he put on a sweater over his T-shirt.

"Perfect weather to go fishing." I wiggled my eyebrows. "Ever been fishing, Lee?"

He shook his head and shoved his cell phone in his pocket. "Never."

Dylan laughed and slapped him on the back. "You ain't lived until you been out on Ty's boat and caught bass. I caught a fish the last time we went out. Fed the entire family for dinner." Dylan put out his hands to show how big the fish had been.

"Really? Where was I?" I asked.

"In Boston," Ty said with a sad smile.

"Well, Lydia and I are here now. Let me put on my bathing suit and tell Justin!" Geri headed back into the bedroom.

"Fishing and lunch on the water? We can grab some snacks and sandwiches before we go," Ty said to everyone.

"Works for me," Lee said with a shrug.

"Does, um, anyone have clothes that Lee can borrow that aren't slacks?" I giggled as I took in Lee's outfit. The pressed chinos were a nice Nantucket red, I at least had to give him that.

"Yeah. We can stop by the house beforehand. I have something," Dylan offered.

"Perfect. It's going to be a good day." Ty kissed my forehead.

"Every day with you is a good day."

"You guys just made me vomit in my mouth a bit. Let's go before you start making out." As if on cue, Geri came waltzing out wearing ripped jeans and an oversized sweater. It hung off her shoulders, highlighting the tattoos that covered her back. I loved the ones on her shoulder the best—two bright yellow sunflowers.

"Don't worry, my bathing suit is underneath." She pulled up her shirt to showcase her rainbow-colored two-piece.

Dylan pulled the straps on the back, sending them snapping back against her bare skin.

"Ouch!" She squealed and rubbed the spot.

"Don't flaunt it then!" Dylan's eyes sparkled. Geri narrowed her eyes at him. It was funny watching the cat and mouse game these two had going on.

"You guys give me whiplash." I chuckled as we walked outside to the cars.

"Better than road rash," Dylan said.

With a laugh, we all piled into cars to get our adventure started.

* * * *

"Put it all in the cart. I want it all," Dylan said as he pointed to the candy at the grocery store.

"I own a candy store," Ty laughed. "We could legit get all of this for free." Dylan looked at Ty like he had five heads. "Speaking of which, I should call Greg and make sure the store is still standing." He stepped aside to where it was a bit more quiet.

Dylan shrugged and swiped his arm, sending multiple Reese's Peanut Butter Cups and Snickers into the cart. "And chips. What kind?"

"I think plain and Doritos. Nacho and Cool Ranch should do," I said, looking at the cart, which was full of junk food more than anything else. I'd forgotten how much Dylan could eat.

"Hey!" Kara, the cute barista from Starbucks, waved her hand meekly as she approached. Her cheeks turned a light shade of pink when she saw Dylan. Why did every girl fall all over herself because of him?

"Hi." I offered a warm smile. No sense in being mean to her. I knew she was flirting with Ty but I couldn't blame her. He was spectacular.

"What are you guys up to?" She peeked into the cart.

"Heading out on the boat for some fishing." Dylan leaned against the cart and I saw his eyes twinkle. Of course he was going to flirt. That's what Dylan did. He made it his mission in life to have women fall to their knees for him.

Geri and Lee had gone to grab Justin and I knew Dylan was having a hard time knowing that he would have to watch Justin and Geri together. Whether he admitted it or not.

"That sounds like fun. I haven't been on a boat yet since I moved here." I watched Kara tuck her hair behind her ears and smile at Dylan.

She was flirting back! As if flirting with Ty wasn't enough.

"Come with us. We have space. And plenty of food." Dylan looked up at me for approval. I shrugged and quickly typed a warning message to Geri. She had no filter. Which meant that if she didn't approve of Kara in any way, it would be known. By everyone.

"Sure, the more the merrier." I offered another smile. If I smiled any more my face would crack.

Ty came up behind me and wrapped his arms around my waist.

"Hey, Kara. Delivering coffee? I could sure use one right now."

"No. I'm off today. But I guess I'm joining you for some boating and fishing? If that's okay. I don't want to invite myself."

"No way. You'll be my guest." Dylan smirked.

Ty leaned down and whispered in my ear. "Geri is going to have a fit."

Kara and Dylan chatted and I spun around so I could look at Ty.

"Whatever game those two are playing is going to end badly," I commented.

"Or with someone going overboard," Ty added with a chuckle.

"My vote's on the latter," I said as I looked at Geri's text message, which had a bunch of question marks.

"All right, everyone's waiting. Let's finish shopping and head out. Kara, you need to grab anything before we go?" I asked, trying to get things back on track.

"Yeah, actually. Getting some sun would be nice. Let me get my bathing suit and I'll meet you guys at the docks in about thirty minutes. That sound good?"

"Perfect," Dylan said before I could reply. She said her goodbyes and headed out. I watched Dylan's eyes not leave Kara's butt as she walked away.

"Dylan, what are you doing?" I pushed the cart down the chip aisle. He snagged a bag of vinegar and onion chips and threw it in the cart. We didn't need those. We didn't need half the stuff that was in the cart.

"Just inviting a person new to the island out for some fun. I'm trying to be friendly." He made a mock shocked look like what I was asking was so far-fetched.

"Friendly my ass," Ty said as he grabbed a bag of Lay's.

"No funny business. Promise!" Dylan held up his hands. The smile that stayed on his face let me know otherwise.

"If you're trying to play games with Geri, don't. Just be a man and tell her what you want." I glared at him.

"Why does everything have to be about Geri? She's made it perfectly clear Justin is the one for her." Dylan clenched his teeth and stomped away.

Ty placed his hand on the small of my back as we continued shopping.

"Well, he just gave it all away. It's clearly all about Geri," I said with a sigh.

"Hey. They'll figure it out. We have to let them work it out on their own."

"You're right. Just sucks because I love them both and don't want to see anyone get hurt."

"That's one of the many things I love about you. You care so much about everyone. You always want everyone to be happy."

My heart dipped. I did want everyone to be happy, but I knew I'd broken Ty's heart when I'd left. I'd broken my own too. I would have done anything to go back and change the past. But I couldn't. No matter how bad I wanted to.

"Are you happy?" I looked up at Ty with tears welling in my eyes.

"The day you stepped foot off that boat, my happiness returned."

Well heck, what was I supposed to say to that? My tears fell. Leaning on my tiptoes, I kissed Ty before we returned to shopping.

I tried not to think of Dylan and Geri, Lee and whatever he was going through. I tried not to think of the fact that on Monday I'd have to return home and step foot in a courtroom when the thought made me sick to my stomach. I wanted this, every day. Shopping with Ty and planning boat trips with my friends. I wanted this island and all the people that came with it because this was my happiness. It was home.

Chapter Twenty

Ty

The water was calm. Only subtle waves gently swept against the side of the boat, rocking it softly. I loved the feeling of a boat swaying side to side. It was like a baby being rocked to sleep.. Although it was fall, the sun was high in the sky, offsetting the chilly breeze. The love of my life was fishing, with her best friend sunbathing even though she'd probably catch hypothermia. Dylan was showing Kara how to drive the boat, her giggles carrying to the bottom where the rest of us were hanging out. This day couldn't be any more perfect.

"Who is she again?" Geri didn't move from her spot on the chair. She was still a bit pissed because Justin hadn't been able to come with us today. Apparently he hadn't said why — or she didn't care to share. All I knew was that she had inherited the stick that had been up Lee's butt earlier and Geri's was a bit farther up there.

"That's Kara. She works at the new Starbucks," I said as I cast out my line.

"She's annoying." Geri flipped over to get sun on her back.

Lydia shook her head and reeled in her empty pole. She was an oddity, a rare woman who could put on a suit and march into a courtroom, but also bait a fishing pole and skin and gut a fish. She'd taught me how to skin a fish and fry it. I remember staring at her as she'd taken a knife and gutted the fish, not batting an eye.

"You have to scale the fish first." Lydia took a knife from her kitchen drawer and pointed it at me.

"That's a butter knife. It's not sharp enough, unless you plan on making a peanut butter and jelly sandwich." I pulled out a larger one.

"Butter knife works best." She smiled at me and started removing the scales. Her hands worked quickly.

I'd fished my entire life but I'd never learned how to gut and scale a fish. I'd catch them and my mother would handle the rest.

"All right, I'll take that larger knife now." She held out her hand. I placed it in her palm and our fingers brushed. A hint of pink surfaced on her cheeks.

Lately, things had shifted between us. When our bodies touched, always by accident, she'd blush, and I'd pretend I hadn't felt her body shudder. I tried my best to hide my feelings, but there was no point. Lydia was turning from my best friend's little sister into a girl I was attracted to. A girl I wanted to be more than friends with.

"Now, cut away from the fish, away from the guts. Like this." With a few motions, she cut the length of the fish. "Voila!"

"You amaze me, you know that?" I stared at her in awe as she rinsed the fish in the sink.

"It's just a fish." She shrugged.

"Nothing is ever just anything with you. You can turn a law book into poetry. A fish into dinner. Is there anything you can't do?" I closed the distance between us and she sucked in a sharp breath.

I was going to kiss her. My heart thumped in my chest and my palms got sweaty. Lydia closed her eyes and I knew this was my chance.

"Lydia Marie Duncan! You better not have gutted that fish on my counter!" Mrs. Duncan's voice carried from the other room.

I let my fingers touch the soft skin on her arm before we separated, the kiss that would have been still lingering in the air.

"Nothing's biting today," Lydia complained as she re-baited.

"Except Geri," Lee said with a laugh. He was watching Lydia and me fish, clearly trying to understand the process. Which baffled me because fishing wasn't something you had to analyze like a court document. It was one of the easiest, most relaxing things to do. Granted, you could be sitting for hours with no bites, but I enjoyed standing on a boat just watching the water.

"Was that a joke?" Lydia laughed and nudged him with her elbow.

"It may have been." Lee winked. "All right. I think I'm ready to try this." He rubbed his hands together and jumped around like he was going into a fight.

"Okay, do your thing. Do you want me to help you cast it out?" Lydia handed him a pole.

"No. I think I can manage." Lee held the pole with one hand before positioning his hands just right. He put it behind his head and with a subtle flick of his wrist, the line went out with a sharp whizzing sound as it cut the air.

"Now you wait," Lydia commented as she leaned over the edge of the boat.

"Don't do that. You'll fall over," Lee said as he went to grab her.

"What do you mean? Don't do this?" Lydia positioned her feet and leaned over, her arms flailing around.

"Stop!" Lee pulled her sweater. "Wait! I feel something." He let her go as the line went taut.

"Pull!" I said as I leaned over the edge where Lydia had just been to see. "Looks like a big one." I couldn't see anything, but I was trying to pump him up.

"So just pull?" Lee said as he held onto the pole for dear life.

"Slowly. You don't want to snap the line," Lydia said with a smile as she stood next to me. "Holy moly, that's huge!" She added to the excitement.

"I'm going to lose it!" Lee yelled as he planted his feet firmly on the ground.

After a few grunts, Lee finally managed to reel it in the fish. It was about the size of the palm of my hand.

A slow clap came from Geri as she laughed. "That's stunning. That should feed my cat."

"Stop it!" Lydia said with a giggle.

"Congrats, you caught your first fish," I said as I took the pole from Lee.

"Is that a fish or a sardine?" Geri commented again.

"I caught a fish!" Lee smiled wide, clearly not letting Geri's comments upset him.

"All right, now take it off the hook." I waved the fish in front of his face.

Lee's eyes widened. "I have to take it off the hook? No way." He shook his head. "I'm not touching it."

"Oh, come on. It's just a little slimy," Lydia teased before taking it off the line and holding it out to Lee. "Just touch it. You caught your first fish. You have to hold it."

Lee sighed and held his hands like a cup. Lydia placed the fish inside. It was still.

"Is it dead?" Lee held his hands away from his body.

"Maybe. We should throw it back in. It's too small to keep anyway," I said, remembering the fishing laws in Massachusetts.

The fish started moving wildly in Lee's hands. He gasped, as he dropped it on the ground. "Oh hell!"

With a laugh, Lydia bent over, picked it up and threw it back into the ocean.

"It moved!" He wiped his hands on the jeans he had borrowed from Dylan.

"Yeah, they do that." I laughed. I pulled two beers from the cooler and handed one to Lee. "To celebrate your first catch."

"Thanks." Lee eyed me curiously. I knew most people would expect me to be all territorial over Lydia, but I had never been the jealous type. What Lydia and I shared wasn't something that could easily be come between, so I wasn't worried. Lee was her friend, she'd made it clear where they stood, and if he didn't respect that, I could always throw him overboard.

Easy. No evidence. I smiled to myself as I took a sip of my beer.

"She's not what I imagined." Lee looked at Lydia as she pulled a lounge chair next to Geri.

"How so?" Okay, if he started professing his love for her, I wouldn't hesitate to weigh him down first before throwing him over.

"Catching a fish with her bare hands? Dyeing the tips of her hair pink? That's just not the Lydia I've known, that's all. Not good or bad. Just different."

Lydia took off her sweater, her pink polka dot bikini top matching the tips of her hair. She smiled at me before lying back in the chair and taking in the sun. Lee was right, Lydia was different. She fished, had pink hair now and did crazy spontaneous things. She was also a kick-ass lawyer with spiky heels and pressed suits. I was so busy trying to figure out which one she truly was. Which Lydia would win out? But maybe she was all of them combined. A perfect mixture of fun and business. The only issue was getting her to realize that she could have both worlds.

Chapter Twenty-One

Lydia

I sat at my mother's kitchen table, the smell of coffee permeating the air. Everyone was at the cottage, hanging out and watching a movie. I'd snuck away to grab some clothes. Really, I just needed a moment to myself. These past days had been filled with nostalgia. My love for Ty had come barreling back and my entire life's purpose, the goals I had for myself, just didn't seem that important anymore. What seemed important was what was on this island.

"Sweetie, what are you doing here? I thought you kids were fishing today?" My mom took a mug down and poured herself some coffee.

She sat down across from me at the table. I noticed how different she looked. There were age lines at the tips of her eyes, gray sprinkled throughout her hair. So much of my life was passing me by and I was oblivious to it all. Too busy going through my own stuff to even take notice.

"Yeah. We did. It was fun. I just needed a minute." I stared at the untouched coffee in my mug.

"You're homesick." She took a sip of her coffee.

"I'm home now." I looked up at her with tears pressing against my eyes. I don't know why I felt like crying but I did. The emotions that swirled within me were so confusing it legit hurt my brain. I was happy to be home. Sad at the same time because my father was gone. I was happy that Ty and I had reconnected. Sad that I had to go back to work Monday, even for a day. I didn't know what way was up or down or where to go. I was lost even though I had a clear path.

"I've never been good at talking to you about life. Your father was always good with that." My mother's own tears fell. "But I'm so proud of you. Do you know that?"

"Mom, I know." I squeezed her hand.

"No. I don't think you do. I always scolded your dad for filling your brain with law books. It wasn't because I didn't think you were capable. It's that you were always my willful child. You dreamed big dreams and I never thought you couldn't fulfill those dreams. I knew you could and then some. I didn't ever want you to leave."

Both of us were crying. My mother handed me a tissue.

"But now that you're out in Boston living your dream, that spark is gone, Lyd. Every time we talk on the phone, it's short and clipped. Joy seemed to gone from your eyes, but after just a few days of being here, it's back. And I can't help but feel that Ty helped put it there."

I blushed and took another sip of coffee.

"Am I right?" she asked.

"Of course you're right. It's always been Ty for me. I just don't know what to do. Do I give up my dream of being partner and come home? Or do I leave behind the only man I've ever loved again?"

My mother shook her head slowly, taking in my words. "I wish I could tell you what to do, but you have to figure this one out on your own, sweetie."

"I wish Dad was here. He always had some profound thing to say that made no sense yet did at the same time."

We both laughed.

"He was a good guy, wasn't he?" my mother said.

"He was the best. I'm going to miss him."

"I already do."

My heart broke for my mother. She and Dad had met on this island. Their love had grown on the beach, in the waves and sand, just like Ty's and mine did.

"Are you going to be okay?" Although I didn't know where I would end up, the thought of leaving my mother alone made me sick to my stomach. When you grow up on a small island, you grow accustomed to always having someone around. She'd had my father. Now she had lost her one constant.

"Dylan's still here. I don't think he will be for long though. Both my kids are falling in love." She smiled and took another sip of her coffee. "And that's a beautiful thing to watch."

"You notice everything, huh?" I smirked as I checked my phone, which had started buzzing.

"It's a mother's job to see everything. We observe from afar and pray you make good choices."

"Speaking of the prodigal son, he asked that I pick up pizzas. I swear he thinks I'm his slave." I stood up and hugged my mom.

"I love you." She patted my arms. "And I'm always here if you need me."

"Thanks, Mom. I love you too." I grabbed my bag, which I had stuffed an outfit in, and headed to pick up the pizzas Dylan had requested.

My mother and I never had heart to hearts, but something about sitting with her, even for just the few minutes that we'd shared, had calmed me. It would all work out. It had to, because I wasn't willing to give up either of my dreams.

* * * *

"Pizza!" I yelled as I opened the door with my foot. The food was balanced on my arm, and it was scorching hot. "Hot! Hot!" I screeched.

Ty ran to help me, taking a pizza off the top while placing a kiss to my lips.

"I missed you," he said as he slid the pizza on the kitchen counter.

I chuckled. "I was gone for an hour."

He gawked at me like what I'd said was ludicrous.

"Too long. I feel like we have a decade to make up for. So you owe me an hour." He slathered my face with kisses. We did have time to make up for, and every second apart was too long. While I enjoyed our time with our friends, the thought of having Ty to myself again was appealing in many ways.

"Come with me to Boston tomorrow," I blurted out as I opened the pizza box.

"Huh?" He stepped back and searched my face.

"I mean, I know I'll be back Tuesday, but I want you to come with me. I can show you around the town a bit. Maybe we can take in some sights. I know it's only a few days and I'll be back to finish out my leave, but I don't want to say goodbye yet." Ty stared at me, unblinking. Okay, I was crazy to ask him to come with me. He owned a business for goodness' sake. There'd be no way that this was possible. I was a lovestruck idiot who'd forgotten how real life worked. People couldn't just up and leave on a moment's notice. I knew that first-hand from when we parted ways ten years ago.

"I'd love to come with you." Ty smiled and my heart started beating again.

"Whew. I thought I misjudged that one. Who will take care of the shop?"

"I have people who work for me, you know? They'll be thankful for the hours." He rubbed my arms.

"As long as you won't be losing business because of me." I averted my gaze to the ground.

"Hey," he tilted my chin so I was looking right at him, "I'd lose anything for you. I made the mistake of letting you go once. I won't do that again. Understand?" Ty's voice was low and deep, the vibrato causing goosebumps to form on my skin. I'd never seen him so serious before but the darkness in his eyes told me he meant what he'd said.

"I understand," I said.

Satisfied with my response, Ty leaned in and kissed my cheek.

While I was flattered that Ty would give up everything for me, I didn't want him to have to. I realized that I'd expected him to leave Nantucket when we were younger, leave everything he knew behind because I'd wanted to pursue my dream. That had been unfair of me to assume or expect. Nantucket was his home. Nantucket was *our* home, and I knew deep down this was where he belonged all along. I had just been too blind to see it all those years ago.

Chapter Twenty-Two

Ty

The shop was slow so Greg and I made a list, to make sure everything was in order before I left him in charge.

"I've opened and closed before. I got this!" Greg shoved a candy in his mouth.

"I know, but I've always just been a quick ride away." Okay, so I was slightly nervous. I wouldn't miss this opportunity to go to Boston with Lydia, but I was nervous leaving things in Greg's hands. He was eighteen, and had never given me any trouble, but this store was my baby.

"And that's why I'll stop in and check on things for you." The door opened and Dylan waltzed in wearing his police uniform.

"Shouldn't you be saving the world?" I teased.

"Always saving the world. Just dropped Geri and Lee at the boat. Need my candy fix." He started filling his arms with candy.

"It's nine a.m. Little early for candy, no?" I quirked my eyebrows.

"Never too early for candy!" Greg exclaimed with a shocked look on his face.

"But seriously. I told Greg he can call me if he needs anything. I've got your back. Go enjoy yourself. Don't worry about things back here." Dylan threw all the candy that he had gathered on the counter. I swear, if I didn't know him I'd think he had five kids hidden somewhere.

"See? We've got this, now go," Greg said as he started ringing Dylan out.

"All right. I appreciate it. Really." Both nodded at me. Shoving my hands in my pockets, I walked down Main Street, watching the cars hobble over the cobblestone road. I loved that Nantucket still had some of the original traits from the Wayland days. The old houses and churches were some of the things that had been restored and left in the name of history. I wasn't a history buff by any means but history is what holds something together. It was often the thoughts of the past and all that a person or town had been through that propelled someone forward.

Like Lydia and me. Our history was what kept us bonded all these years. Even between the distance and heartache, the past was what made us fight for our future.

The streets were much quieter than they had been just months ago, and Halloween was quickly approaching. It was peaceful, but I also missed the sound of kids' laughter and families enjoying their vacations and taking in the beauty of my town.

I made it to breakfast, where I was meeting Lydia before we headed out on the boat to Boston. She waved from the back of the restaurant. She was more dressed up than these past days, with some dressy pants and a red sweater. But the smile she wore was something I knew she had gotten from being here. It didn't matter what she wore, or where she lived, as long as that smile was there, that's all that mattered.

She kissed me, silencing my thoughts of leaving my shop behind and all the worries of what could go wrong. Each time we kissed it was more intense than the last. My hands roamed her body, grasping at her hips and pulling her closer against me.

"We're giving the people a show," Lydia whispered against my mouth.

"Who doesn't love a good show?" I teased as I held out her chair for her.

"Not Mrs. Garrett. She's about eighty and I'm pretty sure she shouldn't be working anymore. We're going to give her a heart attack." Lydia giggled as Mrs. Garrett hobbled around the small diner.

"Here's your coffees." Mrs. Garrett placed them on the table. "And for the record, I'm eighty-two, and my hearing and vision are as sharp as a tacks. My legs are a bit wobbly but they serve me good." She wiggled her skinny, wrinkly finger between us. "Displays of affection are welcome. It's about all the action I get nowadays." She winked and headed back into the kitchen.

Lydia and I burst out laughing.

I watched Lydia finish prepping her coffee. Light and sweet, just like her. Everything she did, it was with a purpose. A mission that only she seemed to know. She studied the sugar as she poured it in. Stirred with slow rhythmic motions. Lydia called to my body and mind with her movements, her smiles. She was perfect. Beautiful. Mesmerizing.

"What?" She cocked her head to the side and smiled at me.

"Are you going to miss all this? The small-town life?"

Lydia rolled her mug between her hands and looked around. "I already do. It's like this is what I've been missing, as crazy as that sounds. I love this life. But I love my other life too. Quite the conundrum." She wiggled her eyebrows and tried to smile. I didn't say anything. I didn't have to. Lydia knew I could tell how she was feeling.

The emotions that settled over us were suffocating, like promises and expectations that neither of us knew what the hell to do with. Lydia fidgeted with the sugar packets that she had just used. I stared at my black coffee like something would jump up and give me the answer to life's ultimate question.

What wouldn't you sacrifice for the one you love?

Lydia glanced up at me as she started stacking the creamers and I didn't need an answer, or anyone to tell me what I'd do. Because I'd do everything for the one I loved. I'd do anything for Lydia.

* * * *

When I said I'd do anything for the one I loved, that apparently included hauling luggage up to her fifth-floor walk-up apartment. There was no breeze, only stifling air that smelled like smog and cigarettes. I hadn't even been here an hour and I missed the ocean.

"I'm sorry. I didn't know the elevator was broken." Lydia wiped her hair away from her sweat-laden forehead.

"It's okay." I lugged the bags behind me as we stopped in front of a door.

"This is me." Lydia messed with the door and gave it a push before it opened.

We walked inside. It was a small place, but cute. I noticed there were no pictures on the walls. No color or anything. Just plain beige and neutral tones.

"I know, it's plain, right? I just never thought to really decorate." Lydia shrugged and took the bags from me. "Follow me. The bedroom is back here. You can take a nap? I don't know. Are you tired?"

We made it to the bedroom and I took her hand in mine. She stilled and let out a staggered breath.

"Calm down." I smoothed back her hair and cupped her cheeks. "No expectations, okay?"

A stray tear fell from Lydia's eyes and I brushed it away.

"Now that I'm back it's like I'm two different people. I feel like I don't know who I am anymore."

My heart was breaking for her. I didn't know how to help her realize what she wanted or who she was. But I'd try because I loved her more than I loved anyone.

"I miss the breeze. The air here is so different than in Nantucket. I never noticed it before. Or I didn't want too."

"You know who you are?"

Lydia shook her head.

"You're the woman I love. The woman who someday, I hope, will be my wife and bless me with babies who are gorgeous like their momma. You're the love of my life, that's all I know. The rest is for you to figure out, baby. I can't do that for you." I brushed the top of her hand with my thumb.

Lydia smiled between her tears. "You want to marry me? Have babies with me?"

I grinned.

"Don't play hard to get now, Ty Rue. You can't drop a bombshell like that on a woman and expect me not to ask questions." She placed her hands on her hips, the sassiness that I loved coming out.

I jumped on the bed, adjusting myself with my arms behind me. With a sigh, Lydia snuggled in next to me and rested her head on my chest.

"Since you're being a pain, I always thought I'd marry you. That our families would be together forever. Wouldn't that have been great? You don't have your parents, though. My dad's gone." I felt her heart rate quicken against me.

"Our future may look different now but it's still ours. Don't be discouraged because the picture's a bit fuzzy. That's the beauty in life, sometimes things turn out differently. Not bad or worse. Just different."

"Wow, that's profound, Ty." Lydia placed a kiss to my cheek.

"Lee said something like that the other day and it really hit home for me. Just because something is different doesn't mean it's bad or worse. It just is. And what we have, baby, it's meant to be exactly how it is."

"Me living in Boston and you on Nantucket?" Lydia sighed and sat up. With a tug, I pulled her back toward me.

"Don't run, Lydia. We'll work it out. We both were so young when you left for college, we couldn't imagine being apart or a solution that would work where we could both live out our dreams. You promised me you'd commit to this until your leave is over. Can you still do that?"

"Yes, Ty. I can do that." With a chaste kiss to my lips, her breathing evened out and I knew she had fallen asleep. I shut my eyes and tried to focus on the days we had together. Nothing beyond that because the thought of her leaving wasn't anything I could fathom.

Chapter Twenty-Three

Lydia

With my briefcase balancing on my shoulder, my shoes digging into my heels and my pencil skirt threatening to ride up my butt, I walked into my office.

"You're back!" Abi screeched as she lunged at me. "Don't ever leave me again."

I laughed as I kicked off my shoes and sat down at my desk. I ran my hands along the mahogany and glanced out the window that overlooked Boston. It was stunning, being able to watch all the people running from place to place. The beautiful skyline and large buildings that stood in the distance. But I didn't get the same feeling I had the first time I'd walked in here. I was resentful. Unhappy. This wasn't where I wanted to be. It wasn't home.

"Can't say I'm happy to be back," I mumbled as I rifled through the stack of messages that Abi had left for me. She was so organized. Everything was color-coordinated by importance and stacked into separate piles by those colors.

Abi gasped and slammed the papers she was holding down on my desk. Pulling up a chair, she sat across from me and frowned.

"What happened to my Lydia? The woman who couldn't get enough of this place and often slept on the couch so she didn't miss a second of work?"

"I buried my father. Rekindled past relationships. I saw that there was a life outside of working twenty-four-seven." I smiled as I thought of Ty waiting for me at home. I'd left him asleep in bed, which had been difficult to do.

"Can't say I blame you." Abi's frown turned into a smile. "I never wanted to be a legal secretary but here I am, living the dream." She skimmed through the papers and we laughed.

"Then why are you still here?" I wondered what would make someone like Abi stay. She had more balance than I did in her personal and professional life and had no trouble telling me it was five o'clock and time for her to go.

"Money. I'm not inherently wealthily. I blame my parents for doing things they love—schoolteacher and firefighter."

"What did you want to do?" I ran my fingers over the desk. Being a lawyer was what I'd always wanted.

"Be a cop. I went to college and majored in criminal justice and law. Tried out for the academy twice and didn't make it. So here I am!"

"No kidding? You wanted to be a cop?" I looked at Abi in her floral skirt and matching cardigan and perfectly manicured nails.

"Yep. Don't let the outfit fool you. I can kick butt." She laughed as she gathered up her papers. I realized there was so much that I didn't know about Abi — the one friend I'd had since moving to Boston.

"Anyways, I better get back to work. Maybe now that you're back and have a new perspective there will be more balance?" Abi shrugged. "Anytime you want to go out let me know. I'm a good drinking buddy."

"Thanks, Abi. For everything."

She smiled and shut my office door behind her.

I looked at the stack of papers and all the messages I had to return. My email kept dinging and I had two hundred and thirty-two messages I hadn't checked. There was no way there would be balance.

Cramming my feet back into my heels, I marched right over to Franklin's office before I lost my nerve.

"Mr. Franklin?" I knocked on the half-open door before I entered.

"Lydia! You're back. Come in. Come in." He waved me in while still looking at the papers that lined his desk. His desk looked worse than mine. He didn't make eye contact with me as I entered, or even when I sat down across from him. His focus was on whatever he was doing in front of him. I thought of how many times I'd done this — half-listened to someone because I was too enthralled with whatever contract or paperwork was in front of me. It wasn't living. It was rude and inconsiderate. People deserved better.

"I'm here to talk to you about the partner position." I cleared my throat, which sounded like I had a frog in it.

He leaned back in his chair, placing down the pen he had been writing furiously with. Apparently, that had gotten his attention.

I held up my hand and shook my head. "I don't know who you were going to pick but I don't want it. I don't want to know.

"I have no balance, no structure in my life beyond working here. I sleep on the couch in my office some nights. I don't go out or anything because every waking second is filled with contracts and the next case." I took in a deep breath.

"You're a good lawyer. You have a keen eye for contracts and business deals. Don't give that up." Franklin tapped his fingers against the arm of his chair.

"I know. I love my job. I do. But I need to live. I don't want to be sixty years old and wonder where my life went."

Franklin leaned forward and rested his elbows on his desk. His desk was much bigger and nicer than mine and I'm sure I could have an office like this someday. But I didn't want it. I wanted the breeze against my cheeks. My toes in the sand. I wanted my home.

"How about we make a deal?" A small smile spread across his face.

"I'm listening," I said tentatively. I rarely interacted with Franklin alone so I had no idea what to expect from this deal he was offering.

"You work from home. Still looking over contracts for us. Little to no travel, only when absolutely necessary."

My mouth was even drier than before. I couldn't believe that he was offering me this. I wanted to scream yes and dance on his desk but I brushed down my skirt and cleared my throat, trying to remain somewhat professional.

"Same pay and benefits?" I questioned. I didn't want to seem too eager, even though I was.

"Yes. That shouldn't be a problem." He nodded his head.

"How about you add in vision insurance and a stipend to get a home office set up and we call it a deal?" I held out my hand for him to shake. I would have taken less pay and no benefits but I knew I was worth it, especially if he was offering me this deal.

"You drive a hard bargain." Franklin shook my hand.

"I'm a good lawyer."

He laughed.

"Please see Tina on your way out and give her your new address. I assume you'll be moving home?" Mr. Franklin grinned. He'd known all along that was where I wanted to be.

"Yes. I will be." I held the door in my hands. "Oh, and I'm done at five every day. No long nights."

He groaned. "Fine." He pointed his finger at me. "But I expect the same level of work and dedication."

"Absolutely. Thank you."

"You earned it. Now get out of here. You have to be in court in an hour. Traffic will be ridiculous."

I ran out of there so fast, not caring that my feet had their own heartbeats or that I could barely breathe. I was moving home and I couldn't wait to tell Ty.

Chapter Twenty-Four

Ty

Stretching, I felt next to me on the bed and found it empty. I reached for my cell phone and saw that it was almost nine a.m. Lydia must have gone into work. Padding out into the kitchen, I smiled when I saw a wrapped plate of food with a note attached to the top.

Ty –
Went to work. I'll be home around lunch time. Be ready to do something fun.
Love,
Lyd

I pulled off the wrapper that was over the food and picked at the eggs and bacon she'd left me. I tried to think of something to do to kill the few hours before Lydia would be home.

I opened the window and the breeze blew the curtains back. It wasn't the ocean breeze, but it'd do.

Walking around Lydia's apartment, it didn't feel like a home. It was barren and empty, the furniture stark white and stiff. It bothered me that Lydia didn't have any pictures on her walls. No traces of her family. No accents, colors or decorations. I smiled and powered up her laptop and knew what I was going to do. If she couldn't go home, I was going to bring home to her.

After scouring Facebook, calling her mother and wandering the streets of Boston to find the print shop and a place that sold beachy stuff, I was back at Lydia's apartment and hanging pictures.

Google is a godsend, as is Siri. That girl hooked me up with directions, even if she had to recalculate five times. I may have ended in a sketchy part of town, on a dead end, and possibly been propositioned, but I survived.

"There. Much better." I stood back to look at the wall that now had various pictures from Lydia's life. Dylan, her parents, us. But my favorite was all of us in high school, including Geri, with our arms around one another. We all were smiling, wearing our bathing suits and the perpetual tans that we'd had in the summer. It had been our last summer together before Geri and Lydia had gone off to college. The most memorable of them all.

"What are you going to miss most about Nantucket?" *Lydia stretched out on her beach towel as Geri flipped like a pancake.*

"The beach. Most definitely," Geri said without lifting her head.

"New York has beaches you know," I chimed in. Dylan was down by the water trying to get some girl's number. The

summer brought tourists and Dylan was always in his element. I had all I needed right next to me.

"Not the same. Mostly lakes. I went to Lake George with my mom and it wasn't this." Geri sat up and propped her sunglasses on top of her head. I caught her eyes welling up with tears. "Sometimes I wonder if going to college is worth it. I'm going to miss you guys so much. Even Dylan, despite how much he gets on my nerves."

I chuckled.

Lydia gave her a sideways hug. "We'll be friends forever. Nothing could tear us apart. No distance or time," Lydia said.

Dylan pointed up to us and the girls he was with squinted. He was clearly trying to get them to hang out with us.

"If he brings any of those floozies over here. I'm leaving." Gone were the emotions of leaving and back was Geri's attitude. She and Dylan had never dated, but tension and feelings lingered between them. Sometimes things were fine, other times it was awkward and difficult to be around them.

"Hey, they could be nice girls," Lydia said, always having to play devil's advocate.

One of the girls pulled at the drawstring of Dylan's board shorts and Geri snorted.

"Right. She's a real keeper, tugging at his shorts like a cat in heat. Well, she can have him because I sure as hell ain't interested in Dylan William Duncan with his smart mouth, insatiable appetite and sense of humor. Or the abs. I hate his abs." Geri snatched up her towel and stormed off. Dylan glanced up and saw her stalking away and ran after her.

"Wow. That was…"

"Interesting?" I questioned.

"I keep asking Geri if there's something between them but she's tight-lipped. Geri is never tight-lipped." Lydia sighed *and lay back down on her towel. I did the same, our shoulders touching, the sun beaming down on our bodies.*

"They'll work it out. Or kill each other first. Both totally plausible."

Lydia smacked my bare chest. "I love your abs," she said as she let her fingers linger.

"Thanks." I ran my hands down them and stilled her hand, bringing it over my heart.

"Do you think we really will be friends forever? Like in ten years, where will we be?"

"Hmm. I think we'll be married with at least one kid. You'll be a lawyer and I'll own a candy store."

"That sounds perfect." Lydia smiled.

"Yeah. Honestly, as long as I'm with you, I'm good with anything that happens."

And I would have been, but I'd never expected her to leave me. For the years to pile up like trash and for those plans and promises to become distant memories. Now she was back and while we weren't married and didn't have children, we could still do all those things, and there was nothing I wanted more.

I looked at the clock and panicked as I laid out a beach throw and added the mermaid lamp that I'd found at the store. I quickly leaned a beach picture I'd bought on the mantel of her fireplace, which was electric — don't get me started on that — and plugged in the ocean-scented PlugIns. These were the world's greatest invention. With a sigh, I plopped down on the couch and looked at my handiwork.

Not bad for a few hours and no idea how to decorate. Lydia's apartment looked like the beach had thrown up on it, but it was better than the plain colors and lack of wall art.

The door opened and I heard Lydia's keys hit the counter.

"Hey, Ty, I'm home."

I heard her toss her shoes on her wood floor and bit back my smile. She hated high heels, even as a teenager, when dressing up and wearing cute shoes was supposed to be the norm. She'd always preferred flip-flops or boots.

"Oh!" Lydia gasped as she entered the living room, glancing around at all the additions I'd made.

"You did all this?" Gently, she ran her fingers over the pictures that hung on her once-barren wall, now covered with familiar faces. She laughed as she breathed in. "It even smells like the ocean."

"PlugIns." I stood up and motioned to the outlet. "I wanted you to feel as much at home as possible. I know you love the ocean but I know you love Boston too."

"How did I get so lucky?" She clutched the blue accent pillow I'd bought against her chest. "You could have moved on and fallen in love with Kara the barista or some other island girl."

"But I didn't." I sat back on the couch and patted the seat next to me. "You were it for me. No matter how many times I tried to move on I couldn't. My heart belonged to you."

"My heart's yours too, Ty." Lydia tucked her legs underneath herself and smiled wide at me.

"You're scaring me. Why are you looking at me like that?"

"I'm just happy. Want to go to the aquarium?" Lydia jumped off the couch. "I want to see the penguins."

I laughed. I loved seeing her so happy.

"Sure, baby, we can go to the aquarium. You might want to change your clothes though."

Gen Ryan

She glanced down at her suit. "Good call. Wait right here." She quickly kissed my lips and bounced away.

She bounced back into the living room and stopped at the pictures one last time.

"It almost feels like home," she whispered as she caressed the picture of all of us in the middle.

Wrapping my arms around her waist, I showed her what home felt like with my hands, my mouth, anything I could. Lydia deserved the world, and I was going to give it to her.

* * * *

"That was so fun." Lydia linked her arm through mine and smiled. "Can we make one more stop before we head back to the apartment? I need to grab a few things."

"Sure." I put the big stuffed penguin I'd bought her on my hip and held her close to me on the other side. It was chilly and night had settled the streetlights highlighting the way. On Nantucket things would be quiet now. Here, cars whizzed by, honking every few minutes. People were bicycling, skateboarding, you name it. I longed for the quiet. The peace.

Lydia led me into a store that was filled with packing boxes and supplies. I stood back as she talked to the guy at the counter.

"Yes, the soonest you have. I'd love to get someone to pack me up as soon as possible." Lydia's voice carried to where I stood.

"Pack you up?" I moved to the counter and looked between her and the guy she was talking to. He shrugged and clicked on his computer.

"I'm moving." She bit her lip and turned toward me.

173

"Where?" My heart dropped. *She made partner. She's leaving me again.* All the words ran through my mind to try to convince her not to go. Love. That was the only one that kept resurfacing. *You love me. I love you.* That had to be enough to get her to stay.

"Well, I was hoping in with you, but if that's a problem I could move in with Dylan and Mom." She fought back a smile. "Although that seems like a step in the wrong direction, but it's fine."

"You're moving back to Nantucket?" I couldn't breathe. My chest was tight, my eyes were leaking. I think.

Lydia leaned in and whispered against my mouth before kissing me. "I'm coming home. Where I should have been all along."

I lifted her up and spun her around, her giggles vibrating through my body.

"Wait." I placed her down. "Your job? You can't leave this. You love your work."

"And that's why I'll be working from home. Our home. Together. I realized that I can have it all, Ty. I can have my dream job, be with my family on an island that has brought me nothing but happiness. I can marry the man of my dreams and have babies that I hope look like him with light eyes and a contagious smile."

"That's a tall order." I brushed back her hair with a smile.

"Oh yeah?" She quirked her eyebrow.

"Yep. But I'm up for the challenge. Particularly the baby part. I'll never turn down practicing with you." I tugged on the pink tips of her hair, and her cheeks turned the same color.

The guy behind the counter cleared his throat.

"I don't want to interrupt, but I need you to sign."
He pushed some paperwork toward Lydia.

With a click of the pen and a flick of her wrist, Lydia
signed to have her life here in Boston packed up so she
could move home. The love of my life was finally going
to be where she should have been all along—by my
side.

Chapter Twenty-Five

Lydia

Today felt different. I wasn't going home for a visit; I was going home for good. My mind wasn't filled with thoughts of work, it was filled with the future, which included the man who had waited ten years for me to realize that following my dreams was important but finding balance and holding onto love was what I had been missing.

"Any regrets?" Ty sat next to me and handed me my ticket.

"None at all. Just thinking about how I've done this trip a thousand times but this feels like I'm going home for the first time. I can't wait to tell my mom and Dylan. They're going to freak out!" I'd opted to not tell anyone that I was moving back home. I wanted to do it in person.

Ty nodded as our boat was called. He picked up my bag and grunted. "What did you pack? The kitchen sink?" He hoisted it over his shoulder.

"I may have put the pictures you made for me in there."

Ty's eyes softened.

"I didn't trust the movers with them."

Ty kissed me on the forehead and I took his free hand as we boarded the boat.

I always enjoyed sitting on the top of the boat, watching the city get smaller and smaller in the distance. It had been my home for the past ten years, and while I knew it had been just a temporary place for me, it had helped me realize so many things about myself. Every part of my life had been a stepping stone. Something I needed to experience in order to move on to the next point. And I was thankful for all my stepping stones, because they'd led me to where I needed to be. Nantucket. I'd needed to experience the big city life, and working for a big law firm, in order to appreciate what I'd run out on.

Ty came up behind me and handed me a beer that he'd purchased from the bar below.

"I thought this deserved a toast." Ty held out his bottle. "To new beginnings and happy endings."

"And to love," I added as we clinked bottles.

"Always, love," Ty said as he brought me close against him. We stayed like this, in each other's arms, as we watched Cape Cod fade into the distance. There was no dread. No heartache or nerves that had been festering for a decade, just the feeling of the arms of the man I loved around me, and the ocean breeze that was taking me home.

* * * *

"Mom! We're back!" Ty trailed behind me as we headed toward the kitchen, where I heard Mom and Dylan talking.

"Hey, sis, how was Boston?" They were eating dinner, my mother's special lasagne.

"Sit! Sit! I made you both spots at the table." Mom got up and started plating us food. "I wanted to wait but you know your brother when it comes to food."

Dylan shrugged as he scooped another bite of lasagne into his mouth.

"Thanks, I love your lasagne." Ty patted his stomach as he took a heaping bite.

"So, Boston?" Dylan quirked his eyebrow. "Did you win the case? Score partner?"

"Oh. It was good. We went to the aquarium. Did a bit of sightseeing. But I had to work so we didn't do as much as I would have liked." I moved my lasagne around on the plate.

"You work too much," my mom said as she sat back down at the table.

"I did talk to my boss about how much I work and all of that."

Dylan and my mother stared at me, waiting for me to continue.

"He's letting me work from home. And no more late nights or any of that." I smiled as Ty took my hand in his. "I'm moving in with Ty."

My mother's eyes filled with tears and she jumped up, her chair crashing to the ground. Before I could blink, I was in her arms.

"You're moving home!" She rocked me back and forth like I was a baby.

"Thanks, man," I heard Dylan say to Ty with a smile.

"Thanks for what?" I asked as my mother still held me close.

"I asked Ty to get you back home. I knew if anyone could do it, it'd be him. You guys were meant for each other. Anyone could see that. Even me, and I know nothing about love." The way Dylan said those last words made my heart ache for him. He knew about love. Despite us always pranking one another and stuff growing up, Dylan was the best, most loving brother ever.

"You wanted me back home?" I could finally breathe as my mom mumbled something and left the kitchen.

Dylan grunted awkwardly and pushed his chair away from the table. "You're my sister. One of my best friends. It's sucky being here without you. Of course I wanted you home. I never wanted you to leave."

I jumped up from my chair and wrapped my arms around Dylan's neck. "You love me! I knew it."

He laughed and patted my arm. "Always have. It's my job though to be a pain in the butt big brother." I kissed his cheek just as my mom re-entered the room.

"Celebration time!" She held a bottle of scotch.

"Where'd you get that?" Dylan asked.

"Your father hid it for a special occasion. I think he'd approve and agree that this warrants as one."

Ty gathered drinking glasses from the cabinet and passed them out.

"I'm so happy! Now you guys can get married!" my mother said and I nearly spit up my scotch.

"One step at a time, Mom." I looked at Ty, who was staring at me, this lovestruck look in his eyes. We'd both been waiting ten years for this to happen. For us to find our way back to each other. So, one step at a time? I wasn't sure when marriage and kids would happen, but it would when it was supposed to because Ty and I did things on our own time, and that was the beauty of love and a bond like we had. There was no rulebook or guidelines. Just two people who fell in love and made it up as they went along. Who had somehow managed to screw it up and put it back together again stronger than before.

Chapter Twenty-Six

Ty

My house was never going to be the same again. All the decorations I'd purchased for Lydia's apartment in Boston were now sitting in the middle of my living room. Lydia was sitting on the floor, emptying each box she had brought from Boston and laughing.

"What's so funny?" I asked as I sat beside her.

"There are just so many things I had packed away and forgotten about. Look at all these pictures of us." Lydia spread the photos on the floor in front of us. There was one of me when I first got my braces, and I looked miserable.

"God, look at my face. That hurt so bad." I rubbed my jaw, remembering the pain of having the braces put on.

"You poor thing." I joked as Lydia rifled through the rest of the pictures.

"I hated you guys for this one." Lydia groaned.

There were Lydia and Geri trying to put makeup on for the first time. They looked more like clowns than anything else.

"You never needed makeup." I reached into the box and pulled out a smaller box that was riddled with stickers.

"What's this?" Hearts covered it, and various sayings about love.

"Oh no!" Lydia snatched it from me and held it against her chest.

"Nope. Give it over." I reached out my hand.

"Fine. Don't make fun of me. I was young!" She buried her face in her hands as I looked through the box.

Everything in the box was from when Lydia and I had started dating. Our first movie ticket. Pictures. Prom tickets. Then I stopped at a letter that had my name and address. It was even stamped.

"I wrote you. Just that once, when I started college. I was lonely." Lydia blushed.

"Can I read it?" I held it gently in my hands. I'd thought Lydia had left and pursued her dreams and never thought about me. That her time in college had been filled with so much happiness that I had been just a distant memory.

Lydia nodded and got up, placing pictures around the living room, presumably where she wanted them hung.

I opened the letter and read.

Dear Ty,
It's been almost five months since I saw you and I thought the pain in my chest would get easier. I thought that I

wouldn't cry myself to sleep every night clutching the sweater I never returned to you. But it hasn't gone away.

The thought of you is there, always, persistent and making me question why I am even here. I'm told that your first love is the hardest to get over. That the pain is something that sticks to you and never lets go. I don't want to get over you, Ty Rue. You are the love of my life and I don't care that you want to open a candy store on Nantucket or that I want to be a lawyer and live in the big city. Our love has to be enough to someday lead us back to each other. Maybe we'll be older, wiser, and more willing to recognize that what we have is the real kind of love that doesn't know time or distance.

Our love is forever.

So, if you find it in your heart, wait for me, because I won't fall in love with another soul. You're it for me. You're embedded in my heart forever.

I love you still.

Lydia

Lydia looked at me as she placed the throw pillows I had bought just a week or so ago on my couch. Tears pressed against my eyes as she leaned into the box and pulled out the sweater that she'd referenced in the letter.

"I never stopped loving you. I was stubborn and foolish to leave but know that my love for you was unwavering. Like the sea." She smiled as she clutched the sweater to her chest.

"Oh, my sweet Lydia," I whispered as I cupped her cheeks in my hands. We didn't kiss. We just stared at each other as the clock ticked in the distance. This silence was what we needed to just feel how badly we wanted and loved each other even after all these years.

Lydia had never stopped loving me and I had never stopped loving her.

"I have to unpack these boxes." Lydia smiled.

"Any more surprises in there that are going to make me fall further in love with you?"

"You never know. I'm full of surprises."

I laughed as she continued to unpack.

I made my way into the bathroom and was hit with the smell of her. Fresh, flowery and delicate. Opening my medicine cabinet, I saw there was perfume and deodorant, a toothbrush and various other items that took up space. She had moved in and I loved that everywhere I turned there was a part of her. Our lives were finally merging together.

"I hope that's okay. I can find somewhere else to put my stuff." I turned and saw Lydia standing in the doorway to the bathroom in her pajamas, her fluffy socks making her feet look two sizes bigger than they were. Her hair was a mess on the top of her head, half falling out of the ponytail thing she had in. She'd never looked more beautiful.

"It's fine. This is your house too now." I closed the medicine cabinet.

"You obviously haven't looked in the shower yet."

I pulled back the curtain and laughed. It was filled with different shampoos, body washes and a giant pink loofah.

"What's this?" I grabbed a big ball-shaped thing off the side of the tub.

"It's a bath bomb," Lydia said. "You put it in when you're taking a bath and there's a surprise inside."

I started running the water and put my hand underneath to make sure it wasn't too hot.

"What are you doing?" Lydia asked.

"I want to try this bath bomb thing. Care to join me?"

Lydia smiled and started taking off her socks.

With a plop, she threw in the bath bomb and lowered herself in.

"I keep the prize." With a crook of her finger, I joined in. And of course I let her keep the prize. Which was a rubber duck. But I got the greatest gift of all, Lydia in my life, every day. No more wondering what our life would have been like if we had stayed together. Because just like Lydia's letter, our love was meant to be.

I held her in my arms, the bubbles and warm water all around us, and I knew no truer words. Our love was one of a kind. The forever kind. And I couldn't wait to see where this crazy life took us.

Chapter Twenty-Seven

Lydia

Months had passed. Yet it seemed just like yesterday that I found Ty again. My life was amazing. I woke up every day to the smell of the ocean, with my arms wrapped around Ty Rue — or a leg, or my entire body.

We were trying to get into a routine but it was hard. Ty's house had only two bedrooms and I didn't want to turn one into an office. Just in case someday we had kids.

My belly fluttered at the thought of having Ty's kids. God, they'd be so gorgeous.

"What are you smiling about?" Ty said as he slid a cup of coffee in front of me.

"Having kids." He raised his eyebrow. "With you."

He brought his own coffee to his lips and grinned. "Not that I'm complaining, but what prompted that?"

"I need an office to work. Filing cabinets. Somewhere to get organized. I didn't want to take the only extra bedroom. For when we have kids." I gulped my coffee, burning my throat slightly.

"I love where your mind is at." Ty kissed my forehead. "What about at the shop? I have a few rooms in the back. One is my office, the other we can make yours. That way we can go into work together every day."

"I wouldn't drive you crazy?" I stood up.

"Of course not. I have to work and so do you. We won't be in each other's hair."

I jumped into his arms, wrapping my legs around his waist. "You're too good to me. But I have a question first."

He laughed and put me down. "What's that?"

"Can I paint it?" I grinned.

"You can do whatever you want with it."

I squealed and kissed him all over his face.

"Who knew I could get all this attention by just giving you an empty room."

I swatted his arm. "I can't wait to get started. I'm going to grab paint today!" I ran into the bedroom and changed into some old jeans and snagged the sweater that I had stolen from Ty all those years ago. When I came out of the bedroom, Ty stood in the middle of the kitchen, his mouth hanging open.

"You're beautiful."

I spun around. "You always say that. I'm wearing crummy jeans and a sweater."

"My sweater. That you stole and never got rid of for ten years. It's sexy as sin." Ty ran his fingers through my hair.

"Careful, you're going to be late," I whispered against his mouth.

"I've got ten minutes. I've been known to do magical things in ten minutes."

With a giggle, I fell onto the couch and found out first-hand just how magical Ty Rue was.

* * * *

"I can't believe you're letting my sister have an office at your store. Work is solace. An escape," Dylan said as he painted the walls of my new office.

"I can hear everything you're saying." I took my paintbrush and ran it down his face.

Dylan gasped, his cheek a lovely shade of pale lavender. "You didn't just do that."

Ty laughed and backed away. "I'm out. I have customers to deal with." He left quickly, before he too became a lovely shade of pale lavender.

"No! You get back here and handle this woman before I do!" Dylan called after him.

"You look pretty." I giggled.

Dylan held the paintbrush he was using away from the wall.

"Don't you dare." I slid back against the wall that we hadn't painted yet.

"Nope. You pay the consequences for what you did. Let's add some purple to that pink hair." Dylan held me down with one hand and put a smear of purple in my hair.

I tried to get free but Dylan was much bigger than me. I wiggled though, which made him start tickling me.

* * * *

More paint was on our bodies than on the walls.

"What the hell is going on here?"

I sat up and saw Geri in the doorway. "You're here? Weren't you doing some big art tour?" I stood up and wiped my hands on my jeans.

"Plans fell through. I decided to pursue my other talent." She shrugged like it was no big deal.

"We're not that kind of town, Geri," Dylan said with a smirk.

"Ass," she mumbled under her breath. "There's a shop for rent down the street. I'm opening my very own tattoo parlor."

"Wow! I had no idea. That's amazing!"

Dylan choked and looked between us. "You're moving home too?" He turned stark white.

"I am." Geri crossed her arms and stared Dylan down.

"That's just great." Dylan threw his paintbrush on the ground and stormed out of the office.

"Wow. Something crawled up his butt," I said.

"Yeah. I'm sure it was a shock to him that I'm moving back. Heck, it shocked me too."

"Well, I'm happy." I grinned. "I'd hug you but I'm covered in paint."

Geri smiled. "I'm so happy for you. Look at this life that you have. It's just going to get better from here." Her eyes welled with tears.

"Are you okay?" I gripped her hand.

"No, but I will be. I know you care about me, and I'll tell you someday what happened between your brother and me, but today is not that day." She pushed back her shoulders and took a breath.

I nodded. This was the only time she'd made reference to something happening between them.

"Well, since you're here..." I held out a paintbrush. "You're an artist, after all."

"I was an artist. I'm just doing tattoos now."

Geri took the brush and immediately started painting, clearly not wanting me to ask what had happened with her art. So I picked up my brush and stood beside her, and in silence we painted the walls of my office.

I didn't know what she was struggling with, but when she was ready, I'd be here for her to help her navigate out of whatever had been bothering her for so long. Geri deserved her own happiness. Just like me. And I knew deep down that although ending up back on the island wasn't her first choice, it'd be good for her. Nantucket had that way about it. It made dreams come true. Dreams you often didn't even know existed. I couldn't wait to see what Geri's new dream would be. Just like her, I was sure it'd be full of color and spunk and every bit of the happiness that she deserved.

Chapter Twenty-Eight

Ty

I'd been riding on a high for the past two weeks. Everything in my life had fallen into place effortlessly. Okay, there may have been ten years that separated Lydia and I, but once we'd seen each other again our devotion and love for each other had been as strong as ever. As planned, she'd moved in with me and we'd fallen into a good routine. She'd made a small office at How Sweet It Is so when I was working, she could be near me. While some people thought we were crazy to do that, we enjoyed spending time together.

Today was one of the biggest parties everyone took part in — Halloween. There were ghosts and vampires milling in the streets, cobwebs and carved pumpkins outside of every house. It was spectacular to see the island transformed. Other than Christmas, Halloween was my favorite.

I'd given a lot of thought to how I wanted to propose to Lydia. There were always the overly romantic ways, like dinner on the beach and an orchestra playing behind us or something simple at home with her family, but I knew that it had to be on Halloween.

How Sweet It Is had hosted the island Halloween party since we opened and I'd always gone in costume. I had to get a ton of people in on the proposal to Lydia, which involved a lot of coordination, but it was worth the headache. Lydia was worth everything.

"I don't understand why you didn't tell me everyone was wearing letters. People are going to think I'm not participating." Lydia stared at herself in the mirror and frowned. She'd decided to go as a cat. She wore a tight black shirt and pants with the cutest little tail. The cat ears stuck up from her head, and I loved her little nose and whiskers the most.

"It's okay. It's your first year back." I tried my best to remain calm. On the inside I was dying. Lydia so badly wanted to be a part of the big island picture, where everyone tried to coordinate. I knew what the costume was, Lydia just couldn't be in on it. Yet.

"Come now. Let's take this picture. I don't have all night," Mrs. Abbott ordered.

"We have to wait for the others." I pleaded with Mrs. Abbott with my eyes to not ruin this. She smiled at me and winked and continued complaining in her typical fashion. She knew she was giving me anxiety and she loved it.

People piled into the shop. Outside there was a block party going on with all the businesses. There was food, decorations and laughter. And most importantly, lots of Scrabble letters.

"All right, before everyone gets drunk and eats themselves into a coma, let's take this picture!" I watched as a bunch of people wearing various letters piled outside.

"Hey. I got everyone lined up. Now what?" Dylan panted and put his hand on his knees to catch his breath. Dylan was taking this all very seriously and wanted it all to be perfect.

Just as Dylan asked, Jack walked in with his parents. He'd had such a big crush on Lydia when he'd met her at story time, I'd known I wanted him to help with this. He was dressed like a wedding ring, and it was adorable.

"Thanks for helping with this." I nodded to his parents.

"Absolutely. Jack was a little upset that he couldn't marry Lydia but he was happy to help."

I laughed. "You ready, Jack?" I took his hand in mine.

"Yes! Let's get married!" he said way too loudly. I glanced around to make sure she hadn't heard, but Lydia was too busy talking to some people at the counter.

"Come outside, Lydia. There's something I want to show you."

Lydia smiled, excused herself from the conversation, and followed behind me.

Outside there was music playing, and I took the microphone as everyone lined up behind me. It didn't make sense at first, but each person who meant anything to her wore a letter, all put together, spelled out Will You Marry Me? I positioned myself at the end of the line as the question mark, and held the microphone as Jack stood in front of me.

Jack looked up at me. "Are you nervous, Mr. Ty?"

"I am."

"Don't worry, she'll say yes." He patted my hand.

People started to gather and Lydia looked confused as she glanced around at all of us. There were her mother, brother, Mrs. Abbott and many others who had touched our lives as we were growing up.

"Lydia, I thought long and hard about when and where I was going to ask you to marry me. And then it dawned on me, what better day than when we would be surrounded by family and friends?" I motioned to the people who stood behind me.

Jack moved toward her and grabbed her hand.

"Since the day that I met you and became best friends with your brother, it was clear that you and Dylan were a package deal. What I didn't realize was that that package was going to be the most amazing thing to happen to me. I fell in love with you, and it tore my heart in two when you left for college. But good things come to those who wait."

Lydia brushed tears away from her eyes.

"Who am I kidding? I don't want to wait anymore. Lydia Duncan, will you put me out of my misery and marry me?"

Jack handed her a T-shirt and she laughed as she flipped it from front to back. One side said yes. The other said no. Each side held the Scrabble points value on it.

Lydia slipped the shirt over her cat costume and I spun her around as I saw the word Yes stretched across her chest. I slipped my mother's wedding ring on her finger.

"Can we take this picture or what? I'm not as young as I used to be!" Mrs. Abbott yelled from behind us. Lydia stood in front of all her family and friends.

"Thank you all for doing this."

Everyone smiled and said their congratulations.

"I think I won this game of Scrabble," Lydia said as she linked her arms with mine.

"How so?" I laughed. "Because from where I'm looking, I won big time."

Lydia looked so happy, and the moonlight and stars highlighted her beauty. There wasn't anything about her that I didn't love.

"I snagged the most eligible bachelor on the island." Lydia winked.

"Nope," Dylan said as he sidled up next to us and shoved a piece of cake in his mouth. "*I'm* the most eligible bachelor." He grinned as he chewed on his cake. It was like a washing machine, watching his food go around and around.

"Eligible bachelor all right," Lydia said with a giggle.

Geri was off in the crowd, and smiled over at us. She and Dylan had been avoiding each other like the plague. Which I guess worked a bit better because it wasn't as easy to get whiplash when around them if they weren't together.

Dylan frowned, but that didn't stop him from shoving more cake in his mouth.

"Well, who won then?" Lydia asked.

"Can we just call it a tie?" I tugged on her shirt. I didn't want her to take it off. Not ever. It was a reminder of the moment everything in my life had made sense. When the heartache didn't seem so poignant, and the ten years seemed like nothing.

Because at the end of the day, I'd gotten what I wanted. Lydia.

"I think that's fair. We both got what we were after." Lydia stood on her tiptoes and wrapped her arms around my neck.

"What's that?"

"A happily ever after." Lydia smiled and pressed her lips to mine.

"Gross. I guess I better get used to that." Dylan gagged dramatically and walked away.

"I'll never get used to kissing you because each time is better than the last," I whispered against Lydia's mouth. "Never thought I'd say this, but you're the best thing I've tasted."

"Better than candy?" Lydia asked through a laugh.

"Better than candy. Loving you is sweet enough."

Lydia sighed and rested her head against my chest.

I wasn't an incredibly wealthy man. I made a decent living running my store, but with Lydia in my arms, I felt like I'd hit the jackpot. I'd give up all the candy in the world if she stayed in my arms forever. And with my ring on her finger, I knew that's where she'd stay. Because I'd been waiting ten years for Lydia Duncan, and I wasn't letting her go.

Chapter Twenty-Nine

Lydia

Every little girl dreamed of her wedding day. The moment when all the stars aligned, when the sun and moon are sitting just right in the sky and she's found the man of her dreams. There'd be a white dress, tons of good food, and music. More than enough drinks to go around and cake that would make even Dylan die of a sugar coma.

I was never that little girl. I always wanted to get married. Especially after falling in love with Ty, but I didn't want anything extravagant or over the top. Which is why I was able to plan my wedding in four weeks. My mother had a fit and insisted that I wait until next year and had some big extravagant ceremony, but all I wanted was the beach, my close family and friends and the man who'd stolen my heart.

"I can't believe you put this together in four weeks." Geri pulled down her light blue bridesmaid dress. One shoulder was bare, the other was long-sleeved and sheer. She looked gorgeous. Her hair was now a pale purple. Gone were the multiple colors that made her look like a rainbow. She was still working on getting her shop up and running, but she seemed happy. As happy as she could be, I guess.

"I know. Feels like I just found out that you were getting married and now the wedding," Abi added.

I didn't have many girlfriends, and all I could think of was having Abi and Geri with me on the day that I got married. Abi wore a different dress that was more form-fitting, but the same pale blue. I was so thankful to have them both by my side today. I wasn't nervous. There weren't cold feet or jitters at the thought of spending the rest of my life with Ty. There was no one else I would want to be my partner in life. He was it for me. He always had been.

"I wanted simple. Nothing too over the top." I stared at myself in the mirror. I loved my dress. I truly felt like a princess. It was silk and satin, the top covered in three-dimensional flower embroidery. My favorite parts were the full bodice and the petal-shaped skirt that was covered in antique silver beads and pearls. The sleeves came right to my elbows. It was perfect.

"You got so lucky with this dress." Geri shook her head and fluffed her hair out.

She was right. I was lucky. I'd stopped in the second-hand shop on Nantucket just for ha-has and this beautiful gown, in the right size, had been hanging with the tags still on it. It had just further solidified the fact that a simple wedding was what I wanted and needed. I didn't need to spend tens of thousands of dollars to make this a day to remember. It already would be because I was marrying Ty Rue.

I'd left Ty and Dylan in charge of picking out their own outfits. All I cared about was that he showed up. He could wear his How Sweet It Is uniform for all I cared. Geri thought I was crazy, but I shrugged it off. Our wedding would be exactly what it needed to be.

I heard the door to my childhood bedroom open and my mom gasped.

"Oh, Lyd, you look gorgeous. Absolutely stunning." Bringing me in for a hug, she stopped and tugged on a piece of hair that was swooping into my face.

"What's this?" she asked.

"Something blue," Geri said with a smile.

The pink was gone from my hair and Geri had added a blue strip that matched their dresses.

"Geri," my mother mumbled and shook her head.

"You love me." Geri wrapped her arms around my mother's shoulders.

"I do. I love all you ladies." My mother opened her arms and we all crammed in for a group hug.

"It's time," Mom said. "It's freezing outside. Only you would get married on the beach in November."

I laughed. "It's a quick ceremony, then we go eat and party."

"Let's go." Geri wrapped her arm through mine.

We all filed out of my childhood bedroom and I shut the door behind me. There were so many memories in this house, in that very room — where I'd had my heart broken, where I'd fallen in love.

"You okay?" My mother stood in front of me, a tissue in her hand and tears already staining her cheeks.

"I'm perfect. Just thinking of all the memories that happened in this house. In this very room."

"There'll be many more. Wait until you have kids. I can't wait to have grandbabies running around here." She smiled and clapped her hands together.

"Let me get married first!" I laughed and brushed away my own tears.

"I know. Don't think of this as the end. It's only the beginning."

"You're right."

"Oh, I almost forgot. This is for you." My mother placed a letter in my hand. She kissed my cheek. "We'll be in the limo, waiting."

I opened the letter and out fell a locket. I opened it up, finding it held a picture of my father and me when I left for law school. His arm was around my shoulder, and he was wearing his Proud Father T-shirt. It had been a token gift for Father's Day but my father had worn the shirt every chance he could. The tears were already falling, but as I looked at the letter, I immediately recognized the handwriting.

My father's.

My lovely Lydia,
If you're reading this letter, I'm not with you on your wedding day. You don't know how hard this letter is for me to write because since the moment the nurse placed you in my arms, you were my little girl. One of my greatest creations.

You had a big heart, and an even bigger drive, but I knew someday Ty would wrangle you in. It scared me at first, watching you fall so hard for someone. But I knew just like everything else you did in life, it'd be forever and you'd do it well.

You were meant to be a lawyer. You were also meant to be with Ty. Those two things were always a constant when I looked at you. So today, as you head off to marry your

Gen Ryan

childhood sweetheart, know that I am walking beside you. I'm in the breeze, the fresh salt air, I'm in the sand that you curl your toes in to feel the coolness underneath.

Don't cry because I'm not there, smile because you, Lydia Duncan, have made me the proudest father. Be happy. Love Ty with all you have and please give your mother grandchildren sooner rather than later because I know she's already harping on you.

I love you, kiddo. Never forget that.

Love,

Dad

I clutched the letter to my chest and felt the breeze come in through the open door. My father was here. He always would be.

"You ready?" Geri stood in the doorway, her eyes softening as she looked at my tear-filled face. "Here. Let me put that on."

"I'm ready now." I took my best friend's hand in mine and walked out of my childhood home and into my future.

Chapter Thirty

Ty

Shoving my hands in my pockets, I waited nervously at the end of the makeshift aisle. There wasn't a runner, or flowers. The ocean breeze would have made sure those wouldn't stay in place. Our family, some friends, and people from the island were all gathered around waiting for Lydia to walk down the beach. They were like a beacon, standing in a row that made an aisle. From our past to our future.

We'd opted for Mrs. Abbott to play the violin. She had been quite a musician in her day, playing in the New York City Orchestra. She'd gotten all misty eyed when we asked her. I'd known that old lady had a heart in there somewhere. There was no ring bearer, or flower girl. Just Abi and Geri. And Dylan. Simple. Sweet. Just like Lydia. Just like our love. I'd never forgotten how sweet it was to love Lydia and to be loved by her all those years ago. That's why I was standing here now, about to marry her. I held onto those memories and replayed them in my mind as often as I could. Lydia was always going to my wife. We'd just had a quick detour to get us here.

Abi walked down first, then Geri. The sun was out, but as soon as Lydia came into sight, with Dylan on her arm, the clouds hid the sun and snowflakes started to fall.

Lydia's smile got wider as the snow clung to her hair. Everyone laughed, as it was the first snow of the season. It reminded me of the first day I'd told her I loved. The day she'd told me she loved me too. Now, on the day we were getting married, the snow surrounded us again.

As Lydia and Dylan walked down, Mrs. Abbott started playing an instrumental version of *How Sweet It Is To Be Loved By You*. Lydia hadn't known I'd arranged this and, as soon as she heard it, tears streamed down her face. When they finally made it to the edge of the beach, Dylan kissed Lydia's cheek and leaned in to give me a hug.

"Promise me you'll take care of her?"

Dylan never had said anything like that to me before. He knew my feelings for Lydia were real. That I'd do anything to make her smile.

"You know I will." I smacked his shoulder. With a nod, he stood behind me, and everyone else seemed to fade away.

"You're beautiful." I smiled and took Lydia's hands in mine. I looked down at Lydia's bare feet as she dug her toes into the sand. She was an island girl, through and through.

"Not so bad yourself, Ty Rue." Lydia hadn't told me what to wear but I'd decided on a regular black tux. I wore a blue tie, though, that matched the single blue streak in her hair.

As the snow slowly fell, and the ceremony started, I was mesmerized by the woman in front of me. I called her beautiful a lot, and she was, strikingly so, but today, of all the days, she took my breath away. It was like jumping into the ocean, the cold water shocking but refreshing. After a few minutes I was hooked, floating around and not wanting to leave. Lydia was my ocean, my solace, my heaven here on earth.

"Today, Lydia and Ty have decided to read their own vows."

I gazed at Lydia, who looked like she was in a perfect daze.

"Ty," Lydia started as a snowflake landed on her eye. I leaned in and caught it on my finger. She blew it away before continuing on. "I don't know what to say to make up for the past ten years that we've been apart. I could say that I thought of you often. That every day I questioned whether I should come home and profess my undying love for you. But I didn't. I couldn't. Thinking of you was too painful because I left behind my best friend, my soul mate, the boy who in a snowstorm told me he loved me for the first time." She held out her hand and caught a few stray flakes. "Instead, I want to tell you today that you always were the love of my life. The man I knew that I would marry and have a family with. Although those years apart were difficult, we grew up, but never apart. We grew more in our love for each other. So, for the years that separated us, I am thankful, because I now know that you are the man that I want to spend the rest of my life with."

Lydia slipped a band on my finger and she smiled through her tears.

I thought of all I wanted to say and the words flowed effortlessly. "It's no surprise that I fell in love with you in a snowstorm and get to marry you in the same. Our love hasn't been easy and like you say, the decade apart did make us grow. But everything I did in that decade was for you. For us. I knew deep in my heart, and so did your father, that we would end up together. My last ten years have been a preparation for this day. For when I finally snagged my best friend's sister, and everything I've been doing in my life since you left made sense."

I added a band on Lydia's finger next to where my mother's ring was. I felt like I was going to pass out, because this was it. The moment I'd been waiting for.

"I pronounce you husband and wife. You may now kiss the bride."

I cupped Lydia's cheeks in my hands and stared into her eyes.

"I love you, Lydia Rue. I promise I always will."

"Shut up and kiss me."

My lips pressed against hers and the breeze that had settled during the ceremony picked up. It was my parents, Lydia's father. They'd all come to celebrate.

Surrounded by cheers, Lydia and I walked toward our reception, hand in hand. My life was complete.

Lydia and I had had a room set aside for us to gather our bearings before we headed down to the reception. Once inside I shut the door and pulled her against me.

"Why, Mr. Rue, I do believe we have guests waiting for us." Lydia giggled.

"Let them wait. I've waited ten years to kiss you whenever I want and now that you're wearing that ring on your finger, my lips, your mouth, always."

I kissed her until she was breathless. Until our chests were heaving with our passion and love for each other.

"Is it always going to be like this?" Lydia said as she played with my bowtie. Our foreheads were pressed together, our lips still inches apart.

"No, sweetheart. It only gets better from here." Our lips found their way to each other again, and again, before there was a knock at the door.

"You guys going to stop humping like rabbits and come down and enjoy the party?" Dylan's voice sounded from the other side of the door.

Lydia giggled and I opened the door.

"Good to see you haven't stolen my sister's virtue yet." Dylan narrowed his eyes at me. There was a playful smile on his face though. That was Dylan. Always a jokester.

Lydia smacked his arm.

"Don't worry. We'll make an uncle out of you soon enough," I said with a wink.

Lydia and I walked down to the reception to have the time of our life with our family, on the island where we'd grown up. Where we'd fallen in love. Where we would start our family and make memories that would intertwine with those of our past. And that was a beautiful thing. A life that was filled with family and friends, all within a quick walk to the beach. Where it all started.

Want to see more like this?
Here's a taster for you to enjoy!

Sag Harbor:
The Billionaire and the Princess
Katherine E Hunt

Excerpt

There is no excuse for this kind of behavior. I've promised, sworn and vowed never to fall for a bad guy again. *Take some time out,* I told myself, *learn the real Caitlyn, love yourself before you love others.* Why, oh why, then, am I half-naked in an airplane bathroom with a frickin' drunken, horny cowboy? Why indeed? He's hot, there's that, like *six-foot-two* hot. *You know what I'm talking about. The type of guy that makes you catch your breath when he brushes past you, hair a little unkempt, jaw a little too sharp.*

In my defense, I've had a very strange year and, frankly, life's gotten really, *really* complicated. Then there's the free alcohol, first time in Business Class... It's all gone to my head. I might be forgiven for getting carried away. *But still, no excuse, Caitlyn, no excuse.*

He traces a solitary finger down the outside of my thigh—my leggings hang off one ankle, dragging on the floor. My other foot, placed firmly on the closed toilet seat, is the only thing holding me up.

I lift my hair, curl it up on my head with my hands, soft lips brush against my neck. "You're so freaking hot," he slurs.

At first, I'd thought he had a Texan drawl until he'd confessed, giggling as the words came out, that he'd stolen the cowboy hat from the guy in the next seat down.

He's not Southern—he's just drunk off his head.

He brushes his fingers up my spine, circling the crux of my neck before gliding over my breasts, past the tips of my nipples, until they stop at the slick gusset of my undies. *Fuck.* For a man who smells like a brewery and has lost the capacity for coherent speech, he's pretty deft with his hands.

Pressing tightly onto my pussy, like it's the only thing holding us up, he fumbles with his trousers, pulling at his belt.

"Do you have a condom?" I ask.

"Uh…shi-it. Maybe?" He tries to grab his wallet with his one free hand and we rock back and forth as he tugs at his pocket.

Is this really happening? It was all going smoothly. Steamy, unexpected, drunken smooch in the corridor, unilateral decision to glide into the bathroom. Semi-naked foreplay.

It's all so serious, all of a sudden. Sex with a stranger. That's a sobering thought. *Is this how I want to start my new life?* It isn't part of the plan, that's for sure.

I've never done anything like this. I'm not an angel, but I've always been the *wait a few days, get to know the guy* kind of girl. Admittedly, they'd all turned out to be Mr. Emotionally Unavailable, Mr. Terrified of Commitment or Mr. Sleeps with Your Friends Plural Behind Your Back, but hey, I'd always kept my side of the bargain.

His fumbles prove fruitless. He takes his hand off me to grab his wallet, falls backward, slams hard into the door and slides to the ground. Turns out I *was* holding him up after all.

I spin around. "You okay?" He doesn't have any visible injuries, but he's a tall man in a small space and his knees are around his ears. He still looks cute though. *God, I need to get laid.* My horny is showing.

"Oh shit!" He says it way too loud. *Fuck, he's going to get us caught.* I'm not sure what the punishment is for kinky stuff in airplane bathrooms, but I know I don't want to start my brand-new life in America in an orange jumpsuit.

"Shh," I whisper, placing my finger over my lips.

"Shh. Hee-hee." That giggle again. He's wasted–like, actually out of it. This is rapidly turning into a very bad idea, not that at any point sneaking around with a man I've just met had been a solid choice. Kissing him? That had been fun, but now it feels a little like taking advantage.

He flicks through his wallet, still sat, half on the floor, legs splayed either side of me. "Shit. I got nothing."

I lean down and put my arms around him. He nuzzles into my neck. *God, he smells delicious.* Whoever he is when he isn't half-naked and hammered, he has incredible taste in aftershave. "Let's get you up."

"Wheeee!" With one hefty yank, he's on his feet. The effort sends my back crashing against the toilet roll dispenser. It's like getting a devastatingly handsome, six-foot-two, curly haired, horny octopus to stand to attention. *Impossible.*

Stepping back to steady myself, I hear a crack. *Shit.* Hopefully, his phone isn't super important because it has just smashed into a million pieces under my foot. I kick it out of sight, sit him down on the toilet seat and pull my leggings back up. My libido is fading. Fast.

I pull up my leggings and put my top back on. "You don't wanna do it anymore?" he drawls, his face downcast.

"I don't think that's a very good idea, do you?" He can't even stand up for a start. God knows whether he can get anything else up.

"You're hot." He snakes his hands up my sweatshirt.

"Thank you. You're very, very drunk." I fasten his belt for him, inciting more giggles, and hand him his wallet, which had flown into the sink. "I think I'm going to go back to my seat. It was very nice meeting you, cowboy. Maybe we'll meet again someday in better circumstances." I might sound like I'm fobbing him off, but some part of me sort of wishes it's true. I most definitely shouldn't. The type of guy who allows himself to get in this much of a state is not boyfriend material. Not for me, anyway. But he's a sweetie, and he's cute when he giggles.

Oh, Caitlyn, you're such a damn pushover.

* * * *

The old lady in the seat next to mine looks very concerned. "Did you hear all that noise in the toilet?"

"Yes. Apparently, some drunk guy fell over."

"Oh dear." She cringes. "Some people do get carried away with the free drinks on these flights. I hope he's all right." She's been reading a guidebook on New York for the last four hours and hasn't even acknowledged my presence, but now that I've got gossip, she's all ears.

"I'm sure he's fine. So where are you flying to today?"

She closes her book and looks at me. "New York." Her eyes widen with excitement. Bless her. She has to be at the very least in her seventies. I see a little of myself in her, always excited by new experiences, no matter how old I get. That's the only way to live.

"Well, yes. I meant for business or pleasure."

"I'm going to see my son. He's got a fancy job in Manhattan, going to show me the sights." She curls her lips into the biggest grin.

"Oh, that's lovely."

Something loud crashes behind us. "Oh dear," she mutters. "What now?"

A flash of white comes racing past our seats. A butt. A very naked butt attached to a very handsome, drunken, giggly cowboy.

"Shit," I whisper under my breath. Maybe I shouldn't have left him to his own devices after all. He turns and waves his not-insignificant appendage at a room full of dozing passengers before a hand reaches through the curtain behind him and pulls his drunken, naked butt into First Class.

"Good lord," she says, raising an eyebrow. "I haven't seen one like that since my Henry was alive."

I turn to her and smile, hiding my deep regret at my rash decision not to get cowboy's number before I'd left him. "Lucky you," I reply.

About the Author

You can find Genevieve curled up reading paranormal romance and romantic thrillers or frantically typing her stories on her laptop.

Forensic Psychology is her trade by day, teaching and molding the minds of college students. Her interest in psychology can be seen in her books, each including many psychological undertones. Although she loves teaching, her passion, her true love, lies in the stories that roam around in her head. Yes, they all come from her mind-the good, the bad, and the totally insane.

She lives in Massachusetts-no, not Boston. With each story she shares, she hopes her love for writing and storytelling seeps through, encompassing the reader and leaving them wanting more.

Gen loves to hear from readers. You can find her contact information, website details and author profile page at https://www.totallybound.com

Home of Erotic Romance

Sign up for our newsletter and find out about all our romance book releases, eBook sales and promotions, sneak peeks and FREE romance books!